Her n

CW01066489

A historical novel

Yema Lucilda Hunter

Sierra Leonean Writers Series

Her name was Aina

Copyright © 2018 by Yema Lucilda Hunter
All rights reserved.

ISBN: 978-99910-54-63-6

Sierra Leonean Writers Series
120 Kissy Road, Freetown; Warima,
Sierra Leone
Publisher: Prof. Osman Sankoh (Mallam O.)
www.sl-writers-series.org
publisher@sl-writers-series.org

Acknowledgements

The following people were of immense help to me: Arnold Gordon, a relation of Sarah Forbes Bonetta, who provided me with useful information, not generally known, Pauline Casely-Hayford, who willingly used her access to university library databases to help me obtain a much needed article, Winston Forde, who emailed me both volumes of *Dahomey and the Dahhomans* by Frederick E. Forbes, and Sunni Smart-Cole, who gave me the full version of James Davies's Yoruba name. I should also like to thank my sample readers, who shall remain nameless. I can always rely on them to point out my mistakes and unclear passages, and to make helpful suggestions for improving my story.

To God be the glory.

PROLOGUE

By the fifteenth century of recorded European history, much had been learned about the movement of winds and tides, and about how to travel across the oceans in ships. Encouraged by their rulers, citizens of the seafaring European countries—England, France, Denmark, The Netherlands, Spain, Portugal—had also learned to build tall, strong, sailing ships capable of voyages to distant lands. Their next move was to explore the world in search of markets for the goods their countries produced. Sea expeditions had already discovered many places previously unknown to Europeans—places like India and China, the Caribbean and the Americas. As a result of the trade they engaged in, the owners of these ships made huge fortunes for themselves, for the kings and queens they served and indirectly, for their countries.

Portuguese sailors were the first to explore the west coast of Africa. Once, one of their ships came to a place where the shape of the mountains the sailors saw in the distance reminded them of a crouching lion. Rumbling thunder (it must have

1

been the rainy season) sounded like a lion's roar, so some ship's captain named the place Serra Lyao—Lion Mountain. The British later changed the name to Sierra Leone. Once the Portuguese sailors discovered that they could exchange firearms, hard liquor, glass and metal utensils for the abundance of ivory, gold, and agricultural produce available in these parts, they set up trading posts all along the West African coast and employed agents to manage them. Gradually they became better acquainted with inhabitants of these areas. They discovered that most of their ruling classes had slaves—mainly convicts, debtors, and captives of war, whom they used for their own wars, and that for centuries they had bartered their slaves for goods brought by Muslims from the northern parts of the continent.

World history has shown us that in spite of the religions they profess, and their level of civilization, humans have treated each other with unspeakable cruelty at some time or other; and not much has changed in that regard. When the European ships' captains—Christians, mind you—realized that enormous profits could be made from trading people, like the Muslims, they did not hesitate to start adding West Africans to the merchandise they took back home.

At first, slaves in Europe were servants of one kind or another; but when Europeans began setting up plantation colonies in the Americas and the Caribbean, it occurred to them that the labourers they needed to plant rice, cotton, and sugarcane, were robust people used to working in conditions of extreme heat; in short, West Africans. Using the sale of West Africans to pay for cotton and sugar and rice from new world plantations became so profitable, that demand soon outpaced supply. No longer content to wait for the merchandise to come to them, Europeans began raiding towns and villages, slave-hunting; and once West African rulers realized how easy it would be to boost their own revenues they, too, began to raid the towns and villages of their enemies.

European slavers transported people, captured or purchased, to the new world chained, shackled, and packed in the polluted holds of their ships like canned sardines. Those who survived the ordeal of that journey, lost the remaining shreds of their dignity when the slavers reached their destination. They were made to stand naked on auction blocks to be poked and prodded like animals; and once sold on, unlike enslavement practised in their homelands, were forced to abandon their languages and stripped of their names. Many suffered unimaginable cruelty from their owners.

It is hard to believe that this crime against humanity went on for four hundred years; that millions and millions of young West Africans were taken by force from their homes, their families and the lives they knew, and that generations upon generations of Europeans, and people of European descent, found it acceptable to treat other human beings in that way, using the excuse that Africans were not fully human. Hard to believe; yet it happened, with consequences being felt to this day. Perhaps even more amazing is how long it took for, otherwise good, people to start campaigning against such wickedness. Eventually, groups of British Christians did start a campaign; but it took twenty years of relentless advocacy for the Slave Trade to be forbidden to British subjects. It was so profitable, you see.

And that was not the end of the story. Africans and continental Europeans were not bound by British laws, nor had slavery itself been abolished outside British territories. There were still plenty of customers for the slavers' merchandise, so business went on as usual.

Under pressure from abolitionists, and out of a determination that no other countries should profit from a commercial activity forbidden to its own subjects, the British government sent the West Africa Squadron of the Royal Navy to attack slave-ships and rescue their captives. These poor souls, known as Liberated Africans, had been seized from various places along the west coast and therefore needed new homes. The men-of-war took them to Sierra Leone, where the British had by this time established a colony for former slaves from Britain, America, and the Caribbean.

Meanwhile, Queen Victoria, the British sovereign of the period, was sending special envoys to persuade West African rulers to trade in agricultural produce instead of people. Some of them agreed to the switch and signed treaties to that effect but, like the British ruling classes

5

before them, the powerful kings of Dahomey resisted giving up the source of their enormous wealth. For many more years they continued to raid towns and villages outside their kingdom, especially those inhabited by the Yoruba-speaking people who had been their enemies for years. That was still the situation when this story begins; and the reigning king of Dahomey was called, Ghezo.

PART ONE
Aina

CHAPTER ONE
A Day Like Any Other

The year was 1848. Slave-hunting marauders still roamed the land. Just outside the thick earthen walls of the small, Egbado Yoruba town of Oke-Adan, boys hurriedly uprooted tender grasses to feed the town's goats. Yam farmers tended their soil heaps, ever on the alert for pre-arranged signals from hawk-eyed lookouts hiding in the dense foliage of mango trees. They gave the farmers and boys time to run to the safety of the town and their own compounds.

On this particular day, the farmers had been working steadily since dawn and so far there had been no alarms. At the town's four gates, sentries were, as usual, collecting tolls from itinerant traders wishing to enter. Within the walls, other townsfolk were going about their business, whether it was tending homestead gardens where they grew peppers, tomatoes, onions and leafy vegetables for home consumption, weaving cotton for garments, making garments, or selling in the market. Like other Yoruba towns, Oke-Adan consisted of a number of walled compounds within the outside wall. Each housed a family, its extensions, and their offspring. They were built around the largest compound of all wherein dwelled their ruler, the Oba, and his own extended family.

It was in the Oba's compound that Alafia, a woman of early middle age, was sitting on her porch, protected from the sun by the deep overhang of the thatched roof. She had washed her daughter's hair that morning and was now about to tame the dense mop with coconut oil and a wooden comb. This child, the youngest of the six Alafia had borne, was just five years old, and almost as precious to Alafia as her own two eyes. She had emerged from the womb with her umbilical cord twisted round her neck, putting her life in danger. For that reason, like all Yoruba girls, who entered the world in that hazardous way, she had been named, Aina.

Knowing that she was about to hurt Aina's tender scalp, Alafia offered to tell her a story while she tackled her hair. Usually, singing was the way she helped her endure the discomfort, and Aina loved to hear her mother sing; but she readily agreed to the change, and settled down to listen. Alafia began her story, speaking slowly in the hope that the comb would have freed the worst of the kinks and tangles by the time she finished:

'Three brothers went to Abeokuta to buy smoked fish for a special soup their mother wanted to cook. Abeokuta was a bit far from their village; they had to cross a stream that flowed out of the Ogun River, then walk some distance, part of it through a forest.'

Aina screwed up her face and squealed as her mother tugged at a particularly difficult knot; even so, already well into the story, she said,

'Mami, they were not afraid?'

'Yes, they were afraid,' her mother said, 'but they were brave boys and had each other for company. They reached Abeokuta safely, found the market and bought the fish.'

Aina interrupted again to ask what kind of fish the boys had bought.

'Em, em… catfish,' Alafia said and went on, 'It was almost dark, by the time they came close to the forest again, and they were *very, very* tired, so they decided to find somewhere to sleep…Yes, their mother had told them they could do that,' she answered in response to Aina's next question.

Far from being annoying, Aina's interruptions delighted Alafia. For one thing, they were helping to prolong the story, and for another, were further evidence that this child had a livelier mind than her siblings. Her first three children, all girls, were intelligent enough; but the one before Aina—her surviving son—could only be described as a dimwit, much to the annoyance of his royal father, the Oba. Being the ruler of Oke-Adan, Alafia's husband had taken it as a personal affront, accused her of being somehow negligent while she was carrying the child and, even after she had weaned the boy, did not allow her near his bed for months. Fortunately, her co-wives had, among them, produced normal boys in quick succession. Their arrival had been enough to restore her husband's good temper and, as a result, her position in his household.

Alafia's story went on,

'The boys came to a small house at the edge of the forest, not far from the point where they had to cross the water. There, they found an old woman with a hundred wrinkles and crooked

11

fingers. She was sitting on a stool beside a fire, stirring something in a pot, and mumbling to herself.'

'Mami, she had no one to cook for her?' Aina asked, and before her mother could answer, added, 'Why was she living alone?'

Aina's surprise was due to the fact that in her limited experience, old people, even women, always had someone to cook for them. Some of them sat under shade trees all day long, smoking clay pipes, chatting and dozing off from time to time. Sometimes their mouths gaped in a way that made the children point and fall about with laughter.

'She was a witch, that's why,' Alafia answered.

'A witch!' Aina gasped as another stubborn tangle made her wince. 'Mami how do you know? And what is a witch?'

Without hesitation, Alafia said,

'Old women who live by themselves are always witches. Witches eat all their family members, even their own children.'

The thought that a mother might one day decide to eat her own children shocked Aina into silence, and for a while she asked no more questions as the story went on.

It turned out that, not realizing that the old woman was a witch, the boys asked if they could spend the night with her. She agreed, and even offered them some of the maize porridge she was cooking. They were all hungry, but the oldest boy remembered their mother's stern warning never to take food from strangers for fear of being poisoned. Before the others could answer, he said all they needed was a place to sleep. The old woman gave them a mat and a country cloth with which to cover themselves, and they lay down and slept. In the middle of the night, the youngest brother awoke feeling extremely hungry and decided to eat just a tiny bit of the old woman's porridge. He took one mouthful, but still felt hungry, so he took another, and another. Before he knew it, he had scraped the pot.

Aina gasped again. 'He ate all the witch's food?'

'Yes, he was so hungry that he forgot what their mother had told them; and he was a greedy boy.'

'Mami, what happened?'

'Be patient. I will tell you. He tiptoed outside, picked up stones and put them in the pot. He was hoping that he and his brothers would be long gone before the old woman discovered that the pot was empty.'

'He did not know she was a witch?'

'Yes. Perhaps no old women lived by themselves in their town,' Alafia said.

By this time, she had finished combing out and oiling Aina's hair, and had begun the much easier task of twisting segments of it into tight little puffs which she secured with black cotton thread. The hairdo would last for two weeks before she had to go through the whole tedious process again.

'The boy was not lucky,' she continued. 'The old woman awoke before they left and because she was hungry, she went straight to her pot. When she lifted the cover and saw stones instead of porridge, she shouted, "What! You boys did not wait for me to offer you food? And you did not leave any for my own breakfast? Ungrateful rascals!"

'All the boys denied taking the porridge, but the old woman knew that at least one of them was lying. She said. " I am going down to the water with you. If you are not guilty, you will cross over safely, but if you are lying…If you are lying…If you are lying, the water will swallow you."

'The two older boys walked with confident steps because they knew they had not lied. The guilty one felt a bit scared, but he was a strong swimmer so he thought he would escape. "Go on," said the old woman when they reached the water. "One by one." 'The first brother had the bundle of fish on his head, but he held on to it with one hand and passed through the water without a problem; so did the second boy. But when the youngest boy got to the middle of the water, something started pulling on his legs. He could not even begin to swim. He kicked, and kicked, and kicked, but it was no use…'

'Mami, the water swallowed him?' Aina asked wide-eyed, her voice hardly above a whisper.

'Yes, the water swallowed him,' Alafia answered without emotion. 'I told you the woman was a witch…Witches have power; and they are wicked.'

She replaced the small gold hoops she had removed from Aina's ears for convenience, and said,

'Now, go put the comb and oil in the calabash inside the house, then look for your oldest sister. I want her to accompany me to the market. Tell the other two to pick onions, peppers, and the leaves for *Efe Riro* soup, you hear?'

'Yes, Mami.'

After that troubling story, and the discomfort of having her hair pulled this way and that, Aina was only too glad to do as she was told.

Alafia's husband had three other wives and fifteen children. That day, it was her turn to prepare a meal for the entire family; not as hard a task as one might imagine. Her co-wives and their older daughters were all on hand to help with preparing the pounded yam, fresh green leaves, hot peppers and other ingredients for the *Efe Riro* soup she planned to cook. She was hoping to find smoked fish in the market, as well as her other purchases. Due to the suppliers' need to avoid slave-hunters, fish had become so expensive that to make it last, most cooks added only tiny pieces to soups to improve their flavour. Even so, it eventually ran out. Fortunately, Alafia found some fish to her liking. She also bought a small quantity of goat meat and before long, the slow process of cooking began.

Life, as she was experiencing it, fascinated Aina: birds chirping her awake in the mornings, the cocks' bright combs, and the way they strained their necks to crow, red-headed lizards, nodding before they skittered away, the antics of her slow-witted brother's pet chimpanzee, the older girls' clapping games. Even water fascinated her when it came crystal clear from the well. But of particular interest was watching the preparation of meals—how the women and older girls arranged the two sets of three enormous stones on which the clay cooking pots would sit; how they made kindling by placing small twigs and dry grass in the space in the middle of the stones; how they lit it and puffed to fan the flames, adding bigger, longer pieces of wood through the gaps between the stones, with more puffing to make the fire blaze. How they lifted the pots onto the stones—one for the soup and the other to boil the yam; the movement of the girls' wrists as they crushed pepper and onions on the grinding stone; the rhythmic thudding as they pounded the cooked yam in a mortar; the girls rolling the thick white dough into balls…And then there was the smell—that delicious aroma that made her stomach rumble and her mouth water till she could hardly wait to dip her fingers in the bowl.

The Oba dined alone, except for his personal guard, and the servant who kept him comfortable while he ate by waving a large raffia fan. The rest of the family had their meals in shallow clay bowls, three for the children and one for the adults. After the meal, Alafia's co-wives pronounced her food delicious, which was the polite thing to do. Like the rest of the children, Aina showed her own appreciation by licking her greasy hands right up to her fingertips. Her mother then supervised the cleaning of the cooking pots and bowls and the sweeping away of ashes from under the fire stones.

Eventually, the shadows lengthened and the older children shooed chickens to their coops, and goats to their pens. It was Alafia's turn to sleep in the Oba's house, so when night fell, she said to her children, 'May *Olorun* and the ancestors keep you safe,' and departed to carry out her wifely duties. Gradually, the sights and sounds of the day died away. The sentries secured the four enormous wooden gates in the outside wall, and Oke-Adan settled down for the night.

CHAPTER TWO
Night Terror

Aina's scalp felt sensitive for some time after her mother had done her hair, especially so when she rested her head on the hard earthen floor, with only a mat and a country cloth for protection. The night was therefore advanced before she stopped tossing and turning and fell into a sound sleep. For that reason, she was slow to respond, when her mother shook her, saying in a low but urgent voice,

'Aina, Aina, wake up, wake up'.

Alafia roused the other children with more violent shakes, and the terrifying news that the sentries had come to report that King Ghezo's soldiers were close to the town. Still barely awake, Aina remained on her mat, yawning; but on hearing the name, 'King Ghezo', her siblings scrambled to their feet with cries of fear. Parents threatened their naughty children with, 'If you don't behave, King Ghezo will come and get you.' It seemed that, although they had done nothing to deserve it, that threat was about to become a reality: King Ghezo was coming to get them. The children's panic surged when, amid yells, wild screams, thudding drumbeats and bursts of gunshots, they smelled smoke and began to cough. Billowing smoke at that time of night could mean only one thing—houses on fire.

Aina was still yawning and drowsily rubbing her eyes. Alafia snatched her up, gripped her hand and made for the entrance.

'Run and hide. Fast, fast', she urged the others; but it was already too late. She had barely stepped outside, when a huge man rushed forward with a yell that made them jump back, clutching each other in fright. The man waved a long straight sword and before they could further react, jerked Alafia away from them and tore off her wrapper. The children screamed; so did Alafia, instinctively covering her breasts with both hands. She begged for mercy but might as well have saved her breath. With swift movements the man tucked his sword between his thighs, slapped her hands away from her breasts and handled them as if to assess their worth. After supplying milk to six infants for two years at a time, Alafia's once splendidly upthrust breasts now hung as loosely as the udders of nanny goats. The man must have found them unsatisfactory for his purpose because his next action was to take up his sword again and with a single, twisting blow, chop off Alafia's head.

Aina's siblings fled shrieking into the darkness, never to be seen again, but *she*, rigid with shock and terror, stayed rooted to the spot, whimpering as she chewed on her knuckles. The man swept her up into his arms and a few minutes later threw her among a group of wailing captives who stood huddled like penned goats.

Who knows why that raid happened when, up till then, Oke-Adan had escaped attack? Perhaps one of King Ghezo's Yoruba slave-soldiers, pretended to be an itinerant trader and persuaded one of the sentries to betray his people with a bribe worth many times the usual toll for entering the town, an assurance that he would be spared, and the threat of a supernatural death if he rejected the deal. Perhaps one of King Ghezo's priests used the same threat to make the slave-soldier undertake such a mission against fellow Yorubas. Who knows? Whatever the truth of the matter King Ghezo's soldiers seem to have had no difficulty entering the town.

******

Aina's mind all but shut down after the horror she had witnessed, so that what happened next barely registered. Imprisoned by hard, sweaty arms, and almost stifled by body odour, she was bounced about in a hammock for what seemed like an eternity. Relief came only during brief rest stops. Dawn had barely broken one morning, when renewed drumbeats startled her from a doze. They were approaching a massive earthen wall with round white objects stuck on top of it at intervals. A wide ditch, bristling with thorny branches, provided added security. Two gateways breached the section of wall facing them. Stout wooden posts held up the thatched roof above them. One gate was open, revealing a vast plain with many houses visible in the distance. They crossed the plain and came to another thick earthen wall. This one, not as high as the former, was decorated on the outside with sculpted and painted scenes of hunting, and of raids on towns, similar to what Oke-Adan had just experienced, and on top of it, more round white objects. Two other gateways, similar to the first, stood side by side. One opened before them. The men on horseback dismounted and the raiding party surged forward, singing. Just inside, hard-faced women, uniformly attired in short tunics and skull caps, and variously armed with clubs, spears, swords, and muskets, stood in line on either side of the way leading forward. They raised their weapons, and sang along with the raiders in high-pitched voices till their leader shouted a command. The singing stopped at once. The raiders made a ceremony of handing the captives over to the leader of the women, then turned and filed out of the compound, singing again.

Aina could barely hold herself up as the armed women shepherded them towards the far end of the compound. A rectangular building, with a wide pavilion in front, and another high thatched roof, took up most of the space on that side of the wall. As they approached it, Aina saw a man in a woven cap and matching robe. He was on a huge chair draped with a richly coloured cloth. Other grim-faced women in skull caps stood guard behind him while, to the left of him, a group of unarmed men in robes sat on lower chairs. When the leader of the armed women came close enough to the pavilion, she intoned a certain word, stretched out on the ground, face downwards, and threw dust on her head; her colleagues promptly followed suit and gestured to the captives to do the same. Everyone remained in that awkward position, even after one of the men on the lower chairs beckoned to the leader. She had a brief conversation with him, prostrated herself before the man on the high chair, then crept backwards on her hands and knees. Her colleagues and the captives followed suit until she stood up. Bits of gravel cut into Aina's knees. The pain brought tears, but she tried hard not to draw attention to herself by sobbing.

A grey-haired man with a beard left the group on the pavilion and came forward. He looked the captives over and put Aina to one side before separating them according to their gender. On his orders, two female warriors led them to quarters elsewhere in that huge compound, while another took Aina to a building occupied by ordinary women. A bath and a bowl of maize porridge followed, then one of the women approached her with a gleaming knife. Aina shrank away, whimpering, till she realized that the woman intended nothing more harmful than cutting off her hair and shaving her head. Not that that was a painless experience. The woman worked so fast that here and there, she nicked Aina's scalp, drawing blood. Several times Aina flinched, but was again too frightened to make a sound.

While she was shaving Aina's head, the woman noticed curved scars on both of her cheeks, close to her ears. She conferred with another woman who muttered, 'Omoba'. It was the only word Aina had recognized since her capture; her mother once told her that it meant she was of royal birth. The two women exchanged knowing glances but said nothing. However, the next morning, one of them took Aina back to the big house, and held a brief conversation on the pavilion with the grey-haired man who seemed to be in charge of captives. On his orders, one of the king's female guards took Aina into the house, which was dimly lit, and smelled strongly of lemon grass. With a few words, she handed her over to another group of

women. They were tacking pieces of brightly
coloured fabric onto a large black cloth, and
chatting away as they worked. Previously, Aina
would have been itching to know what the
women were doing but, in her state of dazed
anguish, she watched them without interest. No
one seeing her lifeless expression and hesitant
steps could have guessed that she was a child
whose liveliness and curiosity had once been her
mother's delight.

CHAPTER THREE
In the Court of King Ghezo

At first dreadful scenes played out before Aina's inner eyes night after night—her mother crumpling to the ground, her life blood spurting from her neck like a slaughtered chicken, the fearsome man kicking away the severed head like a coconut; heaps of dead bodies strewn around as he carried her through the town; flames shooting upwards, ravaging everything in their path. Yells, screams, gunshots, more gunshots, drumbeats pulsing steadily all the while. By the third night, her skin burned with fever. She tossed and turned on her mat, sometimes crying out, sometimes sitting bolt upright, her eyes wild, as she screamed. She grew weak; lay almost motionless, curled up like a newborn baby. The women of the household shook their heads, expecting every breath to be her last. But she had been a strong, well fed child before her ordeal. After several days, her fever broke, her nightmares decreased and, though she cried herself to sleep at night, usually did not wake fully until morning. She began to eat a little and as she regained her strength, her quick brain started picking up Fon, the language of her captors.

For several more weeks no one realized that Aina could understand Fon because she did not say a word. The women of the household speculated that she had either been born deaf and never learned to speak, or had lost the ability after the raid on her village which must have been a shock to her system. Neither conjecture was correct. Speaking Fon was a step towards accepting a new life for which Aina was simply not ready. However, she was far too young to resist change for long, especially since, once she had recovered, she spent most of her time among the chatty women of the household. Some weeks later, she overheard a snippet of conversation which she thought was about her.

'This child, eh…Soon we will have to find a name for her.'

Alafia had not been strict about etiquette when they were alone together, but she had trained Aina never to interrupt adult conversations, so it was without thinking that she said,

'I have a name, ma'.

At any other time, the women would have scolded her for such impertinence, perhaps with a slap on the wrist or cheek to teach her better manners; but they were too astonished to care about her behaviour.

'Ee!' one of them exclaimed, clapping her hands. 'The child understands Fon. What is your name?'

'Aina, ma'.

Word spread at once, and from that day on, though she still cried herself to sleep almost every night, and her nightmares persisted, Aina's life became a little more interesting.

The women sent her on errands. One of them was to take the black cloths on which they tacked pieces of coloured fabric to another section of the compound. There, groups of bare-chested, sweaty men sewed the coloured pieces more neatly on to the black cloths and hemmed their edges. Aina could not help being fascinated by the sights and sounds of that part of the compound. Besides the men who sewed the black cloths, she saw others carving objects out of wood, others weaving strips of multicoloured cloths, while others worked with metals. But for strict instructions always to come straight back to the house, she would have been tempted to linger and watch the men at work, though she would not have dared to ask them questions.

The women never stopped talking as they worked and so, as time went by, Aina received answers to some of the questions in her mind. Through quietly paying attention to the ceaseless flow of conversation, she learned that the man she had seen on that huge chair, was King Ghezo himself, that the women she spent time with were mainly slaves, though some of them were his junior wives, that his compound was part of a big town called Abomey, that there was a market outside the palace walls, as well as a parade ground where his soldiers, both male and female, displayed their prowess with weapons. She also learned that the men to whom she took the cloths were all slaves and had to give King Ghezo everything they made, that the female soldiers were married to King Ghezo, but not allowed to bear children because that would make them less fierce in battle, and that all the people captured from her village had been sold to white men. All her life, Aina had been surrounded only by people who looked like her. She therefore could not imagine what the women meant when they spoke of 'white men.' However, since she was not allowed to speak unless spoken to, she had to contain her curiosity. She also wondered why *she* had not been sold with the others from her town, but again, could not ask until her situation changed.

Among the household slaves was one called Mahoussi who had been assigned the special task of taking care of Aina. They shared a mat in one corner of the big house and, as a result, gradually became close. Much younger than the other women but no longer a child, Mahoussi was sometimes willing to answer Aina's questions during the minutes before they fell asleep. She told Aina that her mother had been captured in a raid similar to the one that destroyed Oke-Adan. She had been heavily pregnant at the time and had not yet given birth when the white men came. As a result, she had only been sold when Mahoussi began taking solid food.

Mahoussi had a pretty face and shapely figure but a badly deformed left foot which made her walk with a pronounced limp. She told Aina that her ugly foot was what had saved her from being sold. She also muttered something about it saving her from being given to the ancestors. Aina asked what she meant, but she refused to answer, saying, 'That was not for your ears.'

'Sis Mahoussi, why are those men who come to buy people called 'white men?' Aina asked one night.

'Who knows?' Mahoussi answered. 'The ones I have seen are not white like yam or cassava. Their skin is like... like... Have you seen chimpanzees? The ones with pale skin.'

'Yes,' Aina said, 'My brother had one.'

'Well, the white men I have seen look like that. Their lips are *thin* and their ears are *big*—just like chimpanzees.'

Aina's muffled giggle encouraged Mahoussi to go on.

'But white men's noses are long and high, not flat like chimpanzees...The ones that come here always have on big hats. People say it is because they are afraid the sun will kill them. Their heads are not strong like ours.'

'Sis Mahoussi, do you think I will see white men soon?' Aina asked, though after Mahoussi's description, the prospect alarmed her.

'Yes; they come here often—to see King Ghezo and to buy people.'

'Will I be sold to white men when I grow big like you?'

'The king will decide,' Mahoussi told her. 'Go to sleep now.'

******

As a consequence of her horrific experience, Aina began to fall ill quite frequently—feverish colds for the most part; but sometimes hacking coughs that left her weak. She suffered one of these infections towards the end of her first year in King Ghezo's court, just as the court began buzzing with unusual activity. It was from her mat that she asked in a feeble voice,

'Sis Mahoussi, what is happening outside?'

'They are getting ready for the king's big occasion,' Mahoussi said. 'Everyone goes to the parade ground to watch, even slaves; but they say I have to stay with you.'

'Perhaps we will go next year,' Aina said.

Mahoussi merely grunted. In the past, she had enjoyed the annual ceremonies and the exhibition of fighting skills put on by King Ghezo's soldiers, especially the women, who were as fierce and as skilled with their weapons as the men. However, ever since she had been put in charge of Aina, it had been her fervent hope that something would happen to prevent their going. The ceremonies included spilling human blood to honour King Ghezo's ancestors and Mahoussi was certain that, but for her illness, a high born child like Aina would have been among that year's victims. She had grown so fond of her little charge that had she been responsible for their meals, she would have found a way to upset Aina's stomach whenever the celebration was due to happen. In their situation she could only hope for a miracle, since they ate what was put before them.

No miracle occurred. Aina was in good health when preparations began for the next annual celebration. She kept telling Mahoussi how much she was looking forward to going outside the compound and watching the festivities. She could not understand why, far from showing enthusiasm at the prospect of some excitement to brighten their dull lives, Mahoussi's expression always darkened when she spoke like that, and why she quickly changed the subject.

PART TWO
Frederick Edwyn Forbes

CHAPTER FOUR
The Gift

Frederick Forbes commanded a three-gun brigantine, the *H.M.S. Bonetta.* The Royal Navy man-of-war had been patrolling West African waters for nearly two years, chasing slavers, rescuing captured Africans and taking them to Freetown for resettlement. As expected of a commander and a gentleman, he had put his heart and soul into doing his duty; but he was now more than ready to sail home to the comfort of his loving, lovely wife and four adorable children. Expecting to be on his way in a few days, he had sailed to the Dahomean port of Ouidah only to hand over one copy of his report to the vice-consul stationed at the British fort there;, the other would go to the Admiralty. To his dismay, the vice-consul handed him fresh orders from the Admiralty: by Her Majesty's command, he was to proceed to Abomey and make one more attempt to persuade King Ghezo to abandon the Slave Trade.

Had he been the cursing type, or a less loyal commander in the Queen's navy, Frederick Forbes would have let out some choice vulgarities under his breath, but he was both a loyal commander and a gentleman, so he simply clenched his jaw and asked whether his favourite interpreter, Antonio Cardozo was available.

'Most likely,' the vice-consul told him.

Half-Portuguese and half-Yoruba, Antonio Cardozo spoke fluent Fon, Portuguese and English as well as his tribal language. He was also an efficient organizer who could be relied upon to have any expedition on its way in the shortest possible time. Relieved that, unlike some other commanders, Frederick Forbes had accepted with good grace what must have been an unwelcome order, the vice-consul sent for Cardozo at once.

The man himself turned up the next morning looking as disheveled as ever in a linen suit that had once been white but was now stained and grimy with sweat and other dirt best left unknown. Greasy black hair curled beneath the brim of a battered straw hat. and unshaven cheeks gave his swarthy face an unwashed appearance.

'Commander Forbes,' he exclaimed, with a grin that exposed a fine set of large, surprisingly white teeth. 'Welcome back. What can I do for you this time?'

Frederick Forbes took the hand Cardozo offered, but kept as much distance between them as politeness allowed. Without appearing the slightest bit tipsy, the man reeked of the gin he insisted was what kept him from going down with one of the deadly fevers that gave the coast its bad reputation.

'I have orders to have another go at persuading that dreadful fellow to abandon the slave trade,' Frederick Forbes said, looking glum.

'I can tell you for nothing that you will not succeed this time either,' Cardozo said with a grunt. 'Selling people brings Ghezo more revenue than he can use up, and successfully attacking his enemies increases his fearsome reputation, hence his power at home. He will never give it up; not unless he's made to...And this is not the best time of year to try. His annual display of power is about to begin. He will be even less inclined to do the bidding of a foreign monarch—and a woman at that.'

'You are probably right,' Frederick Forbes said, 'but orders are orders. I have to try.'

'I suppose you want me to organize the expedition and accompany you to Abomey.'

'Of course. I will take six of my officers with me.'

'That makes eight people needing hammocks, with four bearers per hammock. We also need porters for the luggage; another twenty, I'd say. We'll use women to carry some of the lighter stuff. They are cheaper...I hope you have gifts for Ghezo. On this occasion, more than any other, he will expect plenty of expensive gifts.'

'The vice-consul always has a stock of suitable items handy, and I'll see what I can rustle up from the Bonetta.'

'Guns always go down well,' Cardozo suggested. 'So do swords, cowries, tobacco and rum. Ghezo also likes red wine, expensive fabrics, and any eye-catching items, like embossed goblets...'

'I'll see what I can do.'

In a week, they were ready to undertake the journey. Cardozo had shaved and put on a cleaner suit. Frederick Forbes and his party wore civilian trousers, flannel shirts, and broad-brimmed straw hats, planning to change into their uniforms before their audience with King Ghezo. Well beaten paths now traversed the tropical forest, so it was no longer necessary to cut their way through thick vegetation to reach towns. Even with rest stops after every five miles, and overnight stops in towns along the way, the strapping bearers and robust women Cardozo had assembled covered the fifty-seven miles to Abomey in four days. At Kanna, the town closest to the end of the journey, Cardozo shaved again and changed into a clean linen suit, while Frederick Forbes and his men changed into their uniforms. They used their hammocks on the clean, wide road to Abomey, but descended when they could see the outer bulwarks of King Ghezo's capital. Cardozo told the bearers with gifts for the king to continue with them, and the others where to wait within the town. Once again, Frederick Forbes and his men could not hide their disgust at the bleached skulls displayed at intervals atop the earthen walls.

In a little while they began to hear drums and ceaseless high-pitched singing.

'Oh, I should warn you, Cardozo said. 'There are bound to be human sacrifices. These people believe that by spilling human blood to honour the ancestors, the king's good fortune is assured. The ceremony is known as watering the graves.'

Frederick Forbes and his officers expressed their disgust, but could not help being impressed when they entered the town and saw colourful appliquéd banners, broad umbrellas and large canopies of every hue. Under the umbrellas and canopies sat what appeared to be a large proportion of Abomey's population, dressed in their finest, as well as various visiting Europeans and, to the surprise of the new arrivals, some Liberated Africans, to judge from their attire. One would have thought they would want to have nothing to do with a slave-trading king, Frederick Forbes said to himself. Cardozo led the party towards a raised pavilion splendidly decorated with woven fabrics and appliquéd banners. There sat King Ghezo, a lean but commanding figure. To one side of him sat men in rich robes, with ropes of glass and coral beads around their necks. To his other side sat a large group of women attired in gaudy robes, equally colourful head wraps, and a good deal of glittering jewelry.

'Those are the king's councillors and his senior wives,' Cardozo whispered.

When they came nearer the pavilion they saw that, despite the canopy sheltering it from the sun, a female soldier held a bright red umbrella with a fringe of gold thread over King Ghezo. He had on leather sandals, a simple blue and white robe, a broad brimmed yellow hat with plumes, gold earrings, and amulets. In his right hand, he held what looked like a solid gold sceptre, shaped like an axe. Two armed women with fierce expressions stood guard immediately behind him.

One of the councillors spotted Frederick Forbes and his party. and came forward to greet them.

'It is a pity that you have come so late,' he said as he led them to pay homage to the king. 'You have missed the warriors' display. Our female soldiers showed even greater skill with swords than their male counterparts today...And the king has already gone around distributing gifts to representatives of his people. Very soon they will finish giving him their own presents, then all that will be left to do is honouring his ancestors.'

Even as the councillor spoke, they saw groups of King Ghezo's subjects prostrating themselves in front of the pavilion. They kissed the ground, and threw dust over their heads before handing over their gifts. Frederick Forbes made out gourds, probably containing palm oil, woven country cloths, imported fabrics, cages with chickens, and strings upon strings of the small cowrie shells used as currency. When their turn came, Cardozo bowed low before the king while Frederick Forbes and his men stood at attention and gave him their smartest salutes.

King Ghezo recognized the uniforms before he recognized Frederick Forbes and when he did, seemed genuinely pleased to renew their acquaintance.

'Ah,' he said, waving his sceptre, 'The white queen's messenger. I have my own translator, but you can come with yours. Councillor, let them bring more seats so they can be by me and we can talk. Receive the gifts and find seats for the others…I know why you have come,' he went on once they were settled. 'Let me tell you straightaway; this mission will fail as the first one did. I will not stop pursuing and selling my enemies. And that is my last word on the matter.'

'But your majesty, if you sell palm oil from your many farms you will still make plenty of money.'

'Perhaps; but money is not all I care about. Knowing how much my enemies fear me makes my own people respect me more. That increases my power over them.'

As he interpreted the king's words Cardozo gave Frederick Forbes a look that said, 'I told you so.'

The presentation of gifts eventually ended and a few minutes later a strange sight met the visitors' eyes. Led by a priest bedecked with cowries and charms, and with feathers in his hair, a procession of male soldiers was approaching King Ghezo's pavilion. They came in pairs, scores of them, with huge baskets slung between them. Each basket contained a young man or woman robed in white, and wearing a white cloth cap.

'Those are the slaves about to be sacrificed,' Cardozo muttered out of the side of his mouth. 'Get ready for screams.'

'At least, we won't have to watch them suffer,' Frederick Forbes replied.

Much as he loathed the idea of human sacrifice, in order not to offend the king, he was prepared to pretend ignorance of the fate awaiting the poor slaves; that was until the last basket came abreast of the pavilion and he saw that it contained a child.

Shocked to the core of his being, Frederick Forbes shouted, 'NO', and leapt to his feet. Cardozo tried to restrain him, but he shook off his hand and, to the consternation of everyone around King Ghezo, leapt off the pavilion and grabbed the basket with both hands. 'NO!' he shouted again, forgetting that the bearers knew no English.

The female soldiers guarding the king rushed off the platform after him, and it was all he could do not to scream as they forced his fingers off the basket and twisted his arms behind his back. He said, through gritted teeth,

'Cardozo, tell the king that he cannot sacrifice that little girl. He will have to kill me first, and if he kills me, my queen will send her own soldiers to destroy Dahomey.'

Cardozo did as he was told. For a few moments, a deep scowl furrowed King Ghezo's brow; then he snapped an order. One of the women lifted the child out of the basket and brought her to the pavilion, where she stood sobbing and shaking. The other woman pushed Frederick Forbes forward. The incident had brought some of king's wives and councillors to their feet. They now resumed their seats and awaited King Ghezo's next move. He turned to Cardozo.

'Tell him that he has no right to interfere in our customs.'

Frederick Forbes replied, 'Tell him that he has no right to take the lives of innocent people, especially children.'

'Tell him that *we* do not believe that life dies with a body. It will return in another one.'

Frederick Forbes replied, 'Even if you are correct, which I doubt, it is not our place to decide when another person's life should end, except when that person has committed a terrible crime. These people are innocent. They have done nothing wrong.'

All of a sudden, King Ghezo seemed to tire of the argument.

'Bring the child closer,' he said.

He gazed at her for several minutes, obviously thinking. Then he said to Cardozo,

'Tell him that I am prepared to give him the girl. He is to take her to his queen and say she is a gift from the black king to the white queen.'

Frederick Forbes closed his eyes for a moment, so great was his relief.

'Tell him that I shall convey his message to my queen and, on her behalf, I thank him most sincerely.'

With that, the tension eased. King Ghezo ordered that the child be taken to have her ceremonial clothes removed. When she returned, she had a ragged cloth tied around her, barely long enough for modesty. Frederick Forbes gestured to Cardozo and his officers, asked King Ghezo's permission to leave, and gave him another smart salute when it was granted. They took their departure just when, above the general hubbub, they heard the first screams of the other sacrificial victims.

******

'*What* possessed you?' Cardozo asked as they made their way to the gateway.

'It was seeing who was in that last basket. I have a daughter of about the same age and I saw *her* lying there, not an unknown black girl—my own daughter.'

'You could have got us all killed, you know,' Cardozo grumbled.

'For that, I do apologize. I thought no further than saving the child.'

'So what will you do with her?'

'I am honor bound to present her to the queen as Ghezo requested. I shall take her with me to England. Her Majesty will decide what to do with her.'

'And meanwhile…?'

'I shall have her baptized. There is a Church Missionary Society station in Badagry.'

Cardozo raised a bushy eyebrow. 'I see. You intend to turn her into an English girl; black, but otherwise English…'

'It is my duty, Cardozo,' Frederick Forbes said simply. 'Only by civilizing more people like her can we bring such barbaric practices to an end.'

'Have you ever thought,' Cardozo said after a while, 'that when your rulers send young men to fight wars they, too, are sacrificing the innocent for the good of their countries?'

'That's not the same thing,' Frederick Forbes said with indignation.

'Absolutely the same thing,' Cardozo said calmly. 'Just a different way of doing it.'

'I will *never* accept that. How can you compare us with savages?'

'Whether you accept it or not, it's the truth, my friend…And Ghezo's victims probably suffer much less from having their throats slit with one swipe of a sharp sword, than some of those poor young men fatally wounded in your wars, but who take days to die.'

'A philosopher as well,' Frederick Forbes snorted as they went in search of their bearers.

All that time, the little girl had clung to his hand. Cardozo crouched to assure her, first in Yoruba, then in Fon, that she was safe, but she still kicked and squirmed and screamed when

51

one of the bearers tried to carry her on his shoulders. In the end, Frederick Forbes put her to lie on his chest in his hammock. It caused him considerable discomfort throughout the journey back, but gave him a strange sense of peace.

CHAPTER FIVE
A New Creature

'Solemn little thing, isn't she, Owen?' said Mrs. Vidal when her husband introduced the visitors who had just arrived at the mission house. 'And such melancholy eyes.'

'She has lived through several nightmares, ma'am,' Frederick Forbes said. 'In fact it's a miracle that she is alive and of a sound mind.'

'And those scars on the sides of her face…'

'Apparently, they are what make her people know that she is of royal lineage,' Frederick Forbes explained.

'Pity they couldn't have put them on another part of her body if it had to be done; so ugly,' said Mrs. Vidal. 'And how she must have suffered when her little face was cut, poor thing.'

She continued to stare at the child with pity. The child stared back. This was the first white woman she had seen, and the first person with eyes like the cat that lived on the *Bonetta*.

'Do you know her name, Commander?'

'No idea. Since she was a slave, my interpreter assumed she was Yoruba, but she turned her face away when he tried to talk to her. He never got around to asking her her name.'

'Doesn't matter, really,' said the Reverend Vidal. 'Mrs. Vidal will make her clothes suitable for a civilized child, and as soon as they are ready, I shall baptize her…Any ideas for a new name?'

'I had thought of Sarah…'

The Reverend Vidal gave him an approving look.

'A good biblical name for the new creature she is going to become.'

'Also,' Frederick Forbes went on, 'though King Ghezo gave her to me as a gift for Her Majesty, I thought I would give her my own surname and add the name of my ship, 'Bonetta.'

The Reverend Vidal nodded.

'Sarah Forbes Bonetta…Has a nice ring to it.'

Sensing that she was the subject of the conversation, the little girl moved her solemn gaze from the woman to the men talking over her head. She had not responded to the other white man's gentle assurances that she was no longer in danger, but she had understood every word he said and now felt much less frightened than before. Nevertheless, she still clung to her rescuer's hand.

Mrs. Vidal, was an expert needlewoman but, with speed being of the essence, she sought the help of two other missionary wives to prepare a wardrobe for the child. In a few days she dressed her in undergarments, a simple white muslin dress, a bonnet of the same colour, cotton hose, and soft slippers to protect feet which, after years of walking and running over rough surfaces, had needed no protection before.

'There!' she said, so pleased with the result that straightaway she looked for her box of watercolours and painted a quick portrait of Sarah which she handed to Frederick Forbes.

'My husband says there's a clipper sailing for England tomorrow, and that it will arrive at least a week before you do. Why don't you send a letter to your wife, enclosing this portrait? That way she won't faint from shock when you arrive on your doorstep with a little blackamoor.'

'Oh, my wife takes everything in her stride,' Frederick Forbes laughed, but nevertheless decided to take Mrs. Vidal's advice. If not herself,

Mary would need to prepare their children for a visitor who looked nothing like them. He had told them many stories about Africa and its people, but living in rural Berkshire, they had never seen a Negro in the flesh.

In a few more days all was set for the *Bonetta's* northward journey. The little girl, now called, Sarah, still clung to her rescuer, only acting independently when it came to matters of the toilet. On the way down from Ouijah, Frederick Forbes had shown her, with hand gestures, how to use the commode and washbasin concealed behind a panel in his cabin and, much to his relief, she disappeared behind it as soon as she woke up in the morning and just before she settled down to sleep at night. She continued to reject the cot set up for her, and slept on the floor beside his bed. Sometimes she cried out with fear and Frederick Forbes had to comfort her. She rejected the food set in front of her, preferring to stand beside him and pick morsels off his plate; but she did eat, and showed a particular liking for strongly flavoured foods like cheese, salted pork, marmalade and, once they ran out of fresh oranges, lime juice sweetened with cane sugar which the whole crew took to avoid scurvy. Frederick Forbes assumed that those flavours must have something in common with the food she had been used to among her people. During the day, she sat in a corner of his cabin when she was not accompanying him on his inspection tours of the *Bonetta*.

At first she seemed to pay little attention to the ship itself, or to the sailors saluting their commander as he passed; but after a week or so, Frederick Forbes, who had continued to watch her discreetly, noticed that curiosity was starting to conquer her shyness. She began to touch objects on his desk—his journal; his sextant; his telescope; his ink blotter, his hourglass; photographs of his wife and children. And she sometimes hummed little tunes while doing so, or while sitting in her chosen corner. Time to start teaching her English, Frederick Forbes said to himself, and when the words were not too hard to pronounce, named any objects he saw her touch: 'Cup', he said when she touched his coffee mug, and 'Quill' when she stroked his feathered pen. To his delight he observed that she watched his lips closely as he spoke, then repeated the word in a soft, pleasing voice. Time to start getting her used to being with other people, he thought, and seized on the idea of handing her over to Tommy Clegg, the cabin boy who cleaned his quarters and brought him his meals. He had noticed that instead of her usual practice of trying to make herself as small as possible when one of the officers entered the cabin, Sarah had begun to smile at the lad when he came in in the morning.

Frederick Forbes could understand why Tommy appealed to Sarah. For one thing, he was short for a fifteen-year-old, and slightly bowlegged, hence closer to her in size; and for another, she had heard him whistling as he tidied the cabin. Since then Sarah had been trying, so far without success, to whistle as well as hum. Tommy's low-class accent would never do if the child were to be presented to the queen; but that could always be corrected, Frederick Forbes thought. Tommy would introduce Sarah to the ship's crew; that way she would learn English faster.

'Aye, aye, sir,' Tommy answered when the commander told him to take charge of Sarah during the day and start teaching her English.

'But I warn you; don't teach her any vulgar songs or words. And let me know if anyone is unkind to her or calls her names.'

'Aye, aye, sir,' Tommy said with a grin and stretched his hand out to Sarah. She went to him readily, and just as Frederick Forbes hoped, at the end of her first day among the sailors, she came up to him and said, albeit haltingly, 'My name is Sarah.'

'Good girl,' he exclaimed, so delighted that he hugged her with as much warmth as he would have shown one of his own children.

Within days, he learned from Tommy that the ship's crew had grown so fond of Sarah that they had started calling her 'Sally' for short, had introduced her to Greebo, the cat, taught her to tie sailors' knots, as well as the tunes of several sea shanties. She hummed snatches of them in the evenings, and her vocabulary rapidly increased. She now liked kneeling on the banquette which stretched across the ship's stern beneath his windows. 'Bird' she would cry out joyfully whenever one flew past as she looked out to sea. A most intelligent child, Frederick Forbes concluded; and musical as well. He would do his duty and report to the Admiralty that the African child was a gift to Her Majesty from King Ghezo of Dahomey, but hoped he would be allowed to raise her, if only to disprove the notion, current among slave owners and racist scientists, that Negroes lacked the intellectual capacity to become anything more than servants.

PART THREE
Sarah Forbes Bonetta

CHAPTER SIX
A New Life

It was the first time Sarah had lain on a bed, and off the ground. The bed was soft, with white, sweet-smelling sheets, feather pillows and a light blanket to protect her against the cold, though being late July, it was no colder than Abomey in the rainy season. She had never felt more comfortable in her body; yet, tired as she was, it took her a while to fall asleep. She thought about the events of the day: their arrival at Gravesend docks which had frightened her afresh—too many stone houses, the size of which she had never seen before; too many white people milling around; too much thunderous noise as luggage and cargo were offloaded from the *Bonetta* and other ships; and the huge horses hitched to strange conveyances, which Frederick Forbes told her were called coaches when she asked, pointing. They stood on big round iron things. He told her they made the coaches move easily, and were called wheels. Some of the coaches carried luggage on top of them, while others others carried only people; some carried both. Men in tall, black, hard-looking hats controlled the prancing horses. Eventually Frederick Forbes had put her into a coach, which he said would take them home. Only the peaceful green fields she caught sight of as they went past had reduced the discomfort of being jolted and rocked from side to side for miles and miles. Finally, Frederick Forbes announced, with a glad lift to his voice, 'Winkfield; we'll soon be there,' and indeed, a few minutes later the coach pulled up outside a two-storey stone house.

Frederick Forbes was lifting Sarah down from the coach when a large, black, shaggy dog threw itself at him with manic yelps. Sarah wrapped her legs around him with a shriek, and clung like a baby as the dog continued to yelp.

'Don't be afraid, Sally,' he said, 'Rags is part of the family. Down, boy. Down.'

To Sarah's astonishment, the dog immediately sat on its haunches; but with its tongue hanging out, exposing huge fangs, it was still a frightening sight. It took a few more minutes of reassurance, before she allowed Frederick Forbes to put her down among the white people who had rushed up to them behind the dog. They were much

paler than the white people she had seen before.
A young woman with a soft, smiling face stood
on tiptoe to touch Frederick Forbes's cheek with
her mouth; he held her close for a moment and
smiled into her eyes. He introduced another,
much taller woman as, ' Bella, who looks after us.'
But for the fact that Bella had on a frock, Sarah
would have mistaken her for a man for she
detected no womanly softness around her chest.
Bella also looked as strong as a man and proved it
by starting to drag some of the heavy boxes into
the house before a young man, introduced as,
Watson, joined her. Another, older, woman was
introduced as, 'Cook'. There were little white
people as well—four of them, standing one
behind the other. After exchanging hugs with
their father, they stared at Sarah with slightly
open mouths.

'Come and meet Sarah,' Frederick Forbes said,
and one by one they came forward.

'My name is Edwyn,' said the tallest one.

'Tell him *your* name,' Frederick Forbes
prompted, and grinned when Sarah did as she
was told. The children looked at each other in

amazement, and the older girl, Charlotte, said in a hushed voice, 'She speaks English.'

'Only *some* English, dear,' her father corrected, 'but she learns very fast; you'll see.'

The younger children were Lucy, who was the same height as Sarah, and John who, instead of telling her his name, stuck his thumb in his mouth and gave her an unfriendly look, while pulling at his pale, straight hair. Once the introductions were over, the woman, who Sarah guessed was their mother, said, smiling, 'Come along, dear,' and took her hand.

Everything was so strange—the big dog moving freely inside the house, and the house itself, not as large as King Ghezo's palace, but it had an upper floor reached by climbing many steps; the meal they called supper; except for the rice pudding, topped with jam, to which she had already been introduced on the *Bonetta*, it consisted of something like pounded yam, but with a peculiar taste, little green balls they called peas, and a slice of boiled beef in a sauce that had no flavour at all. She liked the bed, though, and burrowed deeper into it prepared to sleep, only to be robbed of that pleasure by a sudden rush of the kind of memories that still gave her occasional nightmares—the attack on Oke-Adan; her mother's brutal murder; her kidnapping; her terror when one of the female soldiers came to their part of the house on the day of King Ghezo's festival. Mahoussi must have known something bad was about to happen because she began to weep as soon as the grim-faced woman appeared, and wept harder when the woman gave her special herbs and ordered her to prepare a warm bath. Her sobs made Sarah start crying herself. When the female soldier wrapped her in a white cloth and covered her head with a cap, Mahoussi cried out in distress, earning herself a sharp rebuke and a hard slap on her cheek; and she continued to wail as the soldier carried Sarah across the compound to where other people in white sobbed with their hands on their heads. Some hours later, male soldiers had appeared bearing large baskets. Amid struggles and screams and pleas for mercy, she and the rest had been forced into the baskets and their wrists and ankles tied. Terror remembered, as well as anxiety about the future, brought tears to Sarah's eyes and, despite the warm night, she wrapped her blanket more closely around her.

Then she remembered how the Captain Forbes had saved her life and smiled, her tears beginning to dry. In her mind's eye and ear, she again saw Mahoussi's joyful expression when she was brought back to the house; heard her glad exclamation when the female soldier told her to replace the ceremonial cloth with another garment; saw Mahoussi smiling through tears as she called out a goodbye. She also remembered going to the place they called Ouijah; seeing the grey-green ocean for the first time, and that enormous wooden house she had since learned was called a ship. Its constant rocking and creaking had made her afraid to walk till she realized that no one else seemed bothered; having to get into smaller boats to reach the shore. The muscular boatmen had reminded her of King Ghezo's soldiers and would have frightened her but for Captain Forbes's reassuring presence.

She remembered that other place, the one they called Badagry, where the white women made her clothes that almost reached her feet, and put things over her feet, and the ceremony when the other white man spoke some words, poured water over her head and gave her a new name, though she had not realized it at the time. She remembered Captain Forbes's kindness when frightening dreams woke her on the ship, and then she remembered Tommy. Tommy Clegg who had made her giggle for the first time in months, and taught her many new things, including the language she now heard all around her, and how to use a spoon and fork instead of her fingers to eat. She smiled again, remembering Tommy, and that relaxed her enough to fall into a sound and dreamless sleep.

******

Two months later, Mary Forbes said to her husband, 'You were right, Freddie, Sarah learns fast.'

The children had disappeared into the nursery with their governess, Miss Emily Atkins, and the couple were enjoying the breakfast Bella had set out for them in their sun lounge: toast, scrambled eggs, crisp slices of bacon, Seville marmalade, and their favourite Darjeeling tea.

'Her English has improved by leaps and bounds,' Mary Forbes went on. 'In fact I think she now knows more words than Lucy, though they are about the same age; and she has almost lost that coarse accent she got from your sailors.'

'As I knew she would,' said Frederick Forbes. 'What does Miss Atkins think of her?'

'Oh, she's *very* impressed. The other day, she said to me, "Mrs. Forbes, without seeing her sable complexion and woolly hair, I should have thought her as English as the other children. She already knows her alphabet, can count from one to a hundred and do simple reckoning. She even helps Lucy sometimes..." That hair, though, Freddie...It has grown hardly at all but even so, I don't know what to do with it. Our combs don't work.'

'Apply some of my pomade and give it a good brushing. That should tame it; at least get it to lie flat...'

'That doesn't work very well, either; I've tried it. She still looks as if she just came out of the jungle. Good thing we can hide it under a bonnet when we go to church; people stare at her enough as it is.'

Frederick Forbes let out a chuckle.

'Yes, her demeanour and speech are quite at odds with her appearance aren't they; but hair aside, would you be willing to raise her?'

'Yes, if Her Majesty allows it. We would be doing a good deed, and all the children seem quite fond of her now, even Johnny…'

'*And* she has got used to Rags,' Frederick Forbes added with another chuckle.

At the mention of his name, Rags rose from one corner of the room and came to sit beside his master's chair, hoping for tidbits from the table which he only received when his master was absent.

Frederick Forbes was a kindly man but, perhaps because of his military training, believed in discipline. He treated his children with equal firmness, though never with smacks or hard knocks, Sarah discovered, much to her relief. Soon after she joined the family, on separate occasions, he made John and Lucy stand in a corner for thirty minutes with their backs to the room. John, because, in a fit of jealousy, he had kicked Sarah on the shin with a booted foot. He resented the amount of time his mother was spending with her. Lucy, because, for a similar reason, she had spitefully called Sarah, 'blackie' in her mother's hearing. And when Charlotte threw her needlework sampler to the floor because her mother asked her to unpick and redo a row of stitching, he had banished her to her bedroom without supper. He followed each of these punishments with a lecture about unacceptable behaviour, delivered in the presence of the other children. Sarah's English was not yet good enough to understand all that he said, but she grasped his meaning from his stern expression and tone of voice, and resolved never to offend him. Consequently, her behaviour was exemplary; that, added to her sweet voice, love of singing, and the speed with which she learned to play the piano, soon endeared her to the family. In that comfortable and secure situation, memories of her previous existence began to fade, her nightmares lessened further, and the summer went by without her catching a single cold.

However, the end of summer brought changes that needed further adjustments: it turned chilly, she needed warm clothes for playing outside, leaves on the trees turned from green to brown and orange and gold, then began to fall. At first they made a pleasant crunchy sound underfoot but rain, and there was plenty of it, soon made them soggy and slimy. The days grew shorter and shorter; it became chilly indoors as well, so that Bella had to light coal fires in the nursery and sitting-room. She put an extra blanket on Sarah's bed, and between the sheets, a metal container with hot water; and Sarah had to wear woollen socks to bed. She had become much less comfortable in her body, but remained perfectly content till Frederick Forbes received a letter which, unknown to her, he had been expecting ever since he submitted the report of his mission to King Ghezo to his superiors.

It came in a stiff white envelope, embossed with the royal seal, and contained the polite command that he present the African child to Her Majesty the Queen at Windsor Castle at 11 a.m. on Saturday, the 9th of November. Even the house seemed to come alive, so great was the excitement within its walls, for it had been beyond the realms of possibility that any of them would see the interior of Windsor Castle, let alone the Queen herself.

'You are going to see the Queen, Sally,' Mary Forbes told Sarah. Sarah had no idea who that might be except that, judging from the awe in Mary Forbes's voice, a queen was obviously a person of great importance.

Frederick Forbes, noticed her puzzled expression and explained, 'She is like King Ghezo, Sally, but not at all wicked. She doesn't kill people.'

'Can a woman be a king?' Sarah asked.

'In this country, she can, but she is called a queen. Queen Victoria is our second one. Long, long ago we had Queen Elizabeth.'

As Sarah digested that information, Mary Forbes said,

'I'm going to make you a new dress, and a coat and bonnet to match.

'More important, you'll have to teach her the correct etiquette before royalty; how to answer questions, and how to curtsey.'

'I think we can leave that to Miss Atkins, Freddie, don't you? *I* shall concentrate on getting her outfit ready.'

Always eager to please the man, who had not only saved her life but remained the soul of kindness, Sarah grew more and more anxious as her coaching progressed. That, with the change of season, might explain why one morning, just two weeks before the appointed day, Mary Forbes heard an explosive sneeze.

'Oh, dear, what a time to catch a cold, Sally,' she said when she saw Sarah's congested eyes. 'Straight back to bed with you.'

Bella prepared two hot water bottles for Sarah's bed, and it was she who suggested wrapping her head with a scarf for added warmth. Fortunately, despite a fever lasting three days, Sarah's chest escaped the infection. By the following week, she felt hungry enough to come downstairs, seeking solid food.

'I can't believe it was that simple,' Mary Forbes exclaimed when she appeared looking frail, but with her once unruly hair now lying neatly on her head like a cap. In her delight that a solution had been found to the problem of managing Negro hair, she grabbed Sarah's hand and burst into her husband's study without waiting for an answer to her knock. Thrusting Sarah forward with an air of triumph, she said,

'Freddie, look.'

For weeks Frederick Forbes had been immersed in editing journal entries for his two missions to Dahomey. He hoped to have them published and wanted to complete the work before his next call to duty; so it was with a slight frown of irritation that he turned from his desk. However, his expression changed to one of pleasure when he saw that Sarah was on her feet again.

'Well, well, well,' he said, 'Look who's back with us!'

'Look at her *hair*, Freddie,' his wife told him. 'And all it took was a scarf. It was Bella's idea, though it wasn't to tame her hair but to keep her head warm.'

'A perfect example of serendipity.' Frederick Forbes said, with a grin. 'All we need now is for Her Majesty to allow her to remain with us…Let's keep our fingers crossed, eh?'

With a lighthearted laugh, Mary Forbes crossed her middle fingers over her index fingers, waggled them at her husband, and left him to his work.

CHAPTER SEVEN
At Her Majesty's Pleasure

Winkfield was a small place, so the Forbeses usually went about on foot. However, they owned one of those one-horse, closed carriages called broughams. On the appointed morning, Watson, who was both stable-boy and coachman, brought it round to the front of the house and Frederick Forbes, resplendent in his navy-blue dress uniform, climbed into it with Sarah. She was dressed in an emerald green, lace-trimmed velvet frock, with a matching coat and bonnet, and black patent leather boots. The hard boots pinched her wide feet; but when she was not gazing in fascination at the snow outside, she took pleasure in their glossiness which was visible among the fringes of the rug covering her legs.

They returned much sooner than expected, causing Mary Forbes to exclaim,

'That was *quick.*'

'Well, the meeting was fairly brief,' her husband told her, 'and as you know, the castle is no great distance from here in the carriage.'

'True. Hurry up and change, then. We're dying to hear all about it.'

Ten minutes later, Sarah and Frederick Forbes joined the family in the sitting-room, wearing their house clothes.

'Go, on, Sally,' he said, 'you start.'

Sarah opened her eyes and arms as wide as they could go and, deepening her voice for even greater emphasis, said,

'Windsor Castle is biiiiig!'

Everyone burst out laughing; but Edwyn said,

'We all know that, Sally; we've seen the outside. What was it like *inside*?'

'Breathtakingly grand, as you'd expect,' his father answered. 'Extremely high ceilings, embossed wallpaper—red with gold trim, portraits of royal ancestors on all the walls; rich wool carpets and rugs, treasures galore...and *huge* chandeliers; I wonder how they get them clean...'

'I want to hear about your meeting with the Queen,' said his wife.

'Yes, Papa,' Charlotte agreed. 'Start at the beginning.'

'All right, here goes. We were met by Sir Charles Phipps, a rather portly gentleman, and his wife. He is the person who wrote the letter; turns out he is Her Majesty's Keeper of the Purse—in other words, he is in charge of the Queen's money matters. They led us first to a little room to tell us how to behave, which wasn't necessary, then Lady Phipps took us to the Queen's private sitting-room. Her Majesty was there with Prince Albert...'

'What does he look like?' Charlotte asked eagerly.

'Don't interrupt,' her mother scolded. But Frederick Forbes said, 'Not particularly handsome—a high,broad forehead, darkish hair, thick moustache; and I thought he would be taller...Anyway, Lady Phipps made the introductions.' With a fond glance at Sarah, he added, 'Sally curtsied very nicely, didn't you, dear?'

'And then...?' Mary Forbes prompted.

'The Queen asked me some questions about Sally's past, then told Lady Phipps to remove her bonnet and take her closer.'

Mary Forbes turned to Sarah with an encouraging smile.

'And...?'

'She looked at me for a long time and made me turn my head from side to side...She touched my earrings and my cheeks and my hair... I didn't like that very much.'

'I wouldn't have, either,' Mary Forbes said.

'I don't think Her Majesty had ever seen an African before,' Frederick Forbes explained, 'at least not at close quarters. She asked me about the scars on Sally's cheeks and when I told her what they meant, she said, "Ah; so she is a princess of sorts. In that case, she may remain with you and your family, Commander Forbes, but *I* shall be responsible for her welfare and all her living expenses...Did you hear that, Lady Phipps? Kindly inform Sir Charles accordingly...Commander Forbes, I expect her to visit me often with her lesson books, and I should like a photograph of her. Lady Phipps, kindly ask Sir Charles to arrange it."... That's all. She dismissed us soon afterwards. Graciously, of course.'

Lucy wanted to know whether the Queen was pretty.

Remembering the hair drawn severely back from a centre parting and almost entirely covered with a white lace veil, the chubby cheeks, beaky lips and nose below slightly bulging eyes, Sarah solemnly shook her head from side to side, which made everybody laugh. The children's amusement increased when their father peered into Lucy's eyes and said, 'Not *half* as pretty as your mother.'

The following week, Frederick Forbes received a second letter from Windsor Castle. At Her Majesty's request he was to have Sarah taken to the studio of John J. Mayall in London for a photograph. Mr. Mayall had already been told to expect them.

'What lucky girl you are, Sally,' Mary Forbes said when she heard the news. 'J.J. Mayall is the most famous photographer in London at the moment.'

'Yes, very lucky,' Frederick Forbes agreed.

Sarah smiled, but her upturned lips concealed anxiety that the Queen's interest in her was going to make her life less comfortable, not more. She had no desire to visit Windsor Castle again, nor did she look forward to posing for a photograph before a total stranger. It had been bad enough having to sit still while that woman in Badagry made a picture of her.

The trip to London did nothing to lessen her anxieties about the future. Once again she was rocked and jolted in a carriage for what seemed like hours; and as they approached London, the concentration of coaches of every description, of high stone buildings standing cheek by jowl, and of jostling, noisy crowds, frightened her. Their progress slowed almost to walking pace so that pedestrians had time to see who was in the carriage. The necks of some of them whipped round when they caught sight of the well-dressed black girl. Ragged boys stared, and made faces at her. Some of them called out, pointing, 'Look, a monkey,' which made her eyes burn with unshed tears.

Sensing her growing distress, Frederick Forbes said, 'Pay no attention to them, Sally,' and closed the velvet curtains. They haven't seen people like you before, that's all.'

'But why did they call me 'monkey'?'

'They are just ragamuffins; they don't have proper homes to teach them good manners. Pay no attention.'

Nevertheless, Sarah felt great relief when they finally arrived at Mr. Mayall's studio; but it was not the refuge she expected, for as soon as they entered the room, what first caught her eye was a large photograph of a man with a drawn sword. In panic, she clutched Frederick Forbes's leg and hid her face.

'What is it, Sally?'

Sarah pointed a trembling finger at the photograph, then drew it across her throat in a swift motion.

'Oh, Sally… that's just a picture,' he said. 'Nobody is going to hurt you here. You are perfectly safe.'

For the benefit of Mr. Mayall, who was looking on with condescending astonishment, Frederick Forbes said, 'She had a dreadful experience a few years ago and associates drawn swords with people being beheaded.'

'How sad,' Mr. Mayall said; but he sounded uninterested, obviously more concerned about taking a photograph that would please the Queen. The two men managed to calm Sarah enough for her to sit quietly and have her photograph taken. She and Frederick Forbes returned to Winkfield without further incident; but that experience deepened her uneasiness about having to do whatever the Queen commanded.

It was not long after their day in London, that Frederick Forbes received his new sailing orders from the Admiralty: with immediate effect he was to undertake yet another mission to West Africa. The rest of the family were used to his comings and goings and took the news with their usual calmness, but Sarah burst into floods of tears at the thought that her beloved guardian would be absent for months, perhaps even longer.

'He'll be back, Sally,' Mary Forbes said, trying to console her. 'He always comes back.'

'And *we* are here,' said Charlotte who had always been kind.

Sarah's sobs gradually subsided, but such was her sorrow that for the first time since she left King Ghezo's court she cried herself to sleep.

The Queen sent for her again and again. Sarah would have preferred to remain in the cozy nursery with the Forbes children instead of having to dress up in scratchy woollen clothes and ride through snow for a visit to the huge and draughty castle; but no matter how politely worded, everyone knew that the Queen's invitations were orders. At first she felt awkward and self-conscious among the older royal children but gradually began to warm towards the one called Alice; and the feeling of friendship was mutual. Alice was about her age and, instead of asking her questions she could not answer about Africa and Africans as the others did, took her riding around the vast grounds of the castle in the royal pony cart. The two girls had to huddle under thick woollen rugs against the bitter cold outside, but their rides and conversations continued till Sarah fell ill with another, more severe, cold. It confined her to bed for much longer than the previous one and she began to cough. The Queen had to be told. She became concerned enough to send one of her own physicians to examine Sarah at home, and that gentleman, not knowing Sarah's history of frequent colds and coughs, assumed that the severity of her illness was due to the English winter. After listening to her chest, he said,

'This child needs to go back to Africa as soon as possible.'

'But she only arrived last July,' Mary Forbes protested. 'Surely, she will become used to our climate in time.'

'Mrs. Forbes, there is a reason the Almighty made these people's skin so dark. It was in order for them to withstand the sun's burning rays in their natural habitat. Negroes do not belong here.'

'But there are quite a number of them in London,' Mary Forbes pointed out. 'I've seen them.'

'You have seen the survivors; the lucky few. This child has the unusual advantage of having people like you and your husband to see to her welfare, not to mention Her Majesty. That notwithstanding, I still believe she ought to be sent back home and shall advise Her Majesty accordingly. Meanwhile, keep her in bed till she stops coughing; the linctus will help soothe her throat and chest. Good day.'

Mary Forbes thanked him profusely for obliging them with a home visit, but she was feeling far from grateful as Bella showed him out. Like the rest of the family, she had grown attached to Sarah and wondered what arrangements for her welfare could possibly match what *they* were providing. The poor child was going to be returned to that savage place with its deadly diseases, *and* to live among strangers. It isn't fair, Mary Forbes said to herself; it just isn't fair. She considered the physician a pompous so-and-so and, clinging to the slight hope that the Queen would not share his opinion, decided to postpone mentioning the possibility of Sarah leaving them. However, before the end of that month, another letter arrived from Windsor Castle. It informed her that, after several consultations, Her Majesty had decided to accept the recommendation that her protégée, Sarah Forbes Bonetta, should be sent back to Africa to safeguard her health.

Mary Forbes murmured, 'Heaven help her.'

In that regard, the letter went on, the Reverend Henry Venn, Honorary Secretary of the Church Missionary Society, would pay her a visit on the following Wednesday to discuss the matter.

Well, no point putting it off any longer, Mary Forbes thought with a sigh, and sent Bella for the children. As she had anticipated, Sarah wept when she heard the news; so did Charlotte and Lucy. It was therefore to a unhappy household that the Reverend Venn came on the appointed day. What he told Mary Forbes over salmon and cucumber sandwiches, washed down with a delicately flavoured tea, reduced some of her misgivings but not her sadness.

'The missionary arm of the Church of England has recently established two educational institutions for the children of Africans we rescued from slave ships and resettled in Her Majesty's colony in Sierra Leone.' he said. 'We hope that with a good education they will one day help uplift their people and bring them to Christ.'

'A noble mission, indeed,' Mary Forbes said. 'Unlike those racists who think Negroes are an innately backward people, my husband strongly believes that in most cases, all they need is a sound education based on Christian values. Our experience with Sarah has confirmed him in his opinion.'

'For the majority of the race, that remains to be seen; but I am hopeful,' said the Reverend Venn. 'As you have probably heard from your husband, the climate is unhealthy in the extreme, and amenities few; but we are making progress— slow but steady progress. Already we have an institution turning out Liberated African teachers and catechists to further our work and, as I told you, we have established two educational institutions for their children.'

'So Sarah is to be enrolled in one of them?'

'Yes,' said the Reverend Venn, obviously savouring the tea and sandwiches. 'Her Majesty requested that I arrange for her to attend the female institution. We do not normally accept children who are not the offspring of formally married Christian parents, but in this case I had to agree.'

'Of course.'

'The school is just two years old, but headed by a female missionary of immense energy and impeccable credentials—Miss Julia Sass. Sarah will be a boarder, therefore well looked after and protected...'

'And how soon will she be leaving us?'

'Probably not for several months yet. We have to identify a suitable adult to accompany her on the voyage; but I think you should start making preparations.'

******

'But I want to stay *here*,' Sarah said, tears welling up again when she knew that her departure was now certain.

'And *I* want her to stay,' Lucy whined. 'Who will help me with my lessons?'

'Darling, I, too, would love for Sally to stay, but we cannot disobey the Queen's orders; we simply can't.'

To comfort herself, as much as the children, Mary Forbes gathered Sarah and Lucy to her. 'Cheer up,' she said. 'It's going to be all right. I'm sure Her Majesty will allow Sally to come for a visit before too long.'

The Queen summoned Sarah to the castle several times in connection with a new wardrobe suitable for the tropics. Bella always accompanied her. On their return to Winkfield one afternoon late in March, Mary Forbes opened the door to them in tears, her face drained of colour.

'Oh, Bella,' she said, her lips quivering, 'we received terrible news while you were away—the worst. Captain Forbes isn't ever coming back.'

Too stunned to speak, Bella clutched at her throat, but Sarah pushed past the two women and ran into the sitting-room, yelling, 'It's not true; it's not true.'

All the children were there. The girls looked crushed, with tearstained cheeks. Edwyn said in a listless voice,

'It's true, Sally. The Admiralty people came to tell Mama when you were at the castle.'

Dry-eyed but pale as flour, he was sitting in his father's favourite chair, with Rags lying at his feet. The dog looked despondent, sensing unhappiness. Sarah sank to the ground, sobbing. Charlotte and Lucy started sobbing again, while John pulled at his hair, sucking hard on his thumb. Mary Forbes had rushed into the parlour after Sarah. She picked her up and brought her to sit on her lap, whispering words of comfort when her own heart was breaking. She could not stop a fresh surge of tears and, for several minutes, the whole family, except for Johnny and Edwyn, gave full rein to their sorrow. Bella had lingered and was the first to regain her composure.

'Ma'am,' she said hesitantly, 'if I may ask, what happened to Captain Forbes?'

'He fell ill, Bella. One of those dreadful fevers people get in those parts. The Admiralty say the ship's surgeon did his utmost but could not save him.'

'Poor Captain Forbes,' Bella sighed, tearful again, 'So young.'

'Yes, so young, my poor darling. And we won't be able to lay him to rest in our churchyard. He was buried at sea.'

In a few weeks, daffodils carpeted the lawn outside the house, signalling the end of winter; but that year their cheerful presence lifted no spirits in the Forbes household. Captain Forbes had remained Sarah's favourite member of the family. With no expectation of ever seeing him again, she resigned herself to leaving England and relieved her sorrow by practising her favourite piano pieces to perfection. And, to the delight of the Queen, she showed even greater progress with mastering English grammar and arithmetic. On the Monday after Easter, the Reverend Venn paid Mary Forbes another visit, accompanied this time by another man in a clerical collar, whom he introduced as the Reverend Schmid. Reverend Schmid was going out to Sierra Leone on his first sojourn as a missionary. He and his wife would be Sarah's companions on board the steam ship, *Bathurst,* due to sail on the 17th of May.

It seemed to Sarah that hardly any time passed before two trunks, crammed with new clothes and presents from the Queen and the Forbeses, were being loaded onto a hired coach for the trip to Plymouth docks. Only Mary Forbes went to see her off. It was a tearful parting.

PART FOUR
The Female Institution

CHAPTER EIGHT
The Reluctant Returnee

It was fortunate that Sarah and her traveling companions had strong stomachs, for though more stable than the *Bonetta*, the *Bathurst* rocked and rolled on rough seas till they passed the Canary Islands and entered tropical waters. When they were not walking the decks, or having meals, the Reverend and Mrs Schmid spent a good deal of time on their knees petitioning the Almighty to bless their mission and protect them from harm; and Sarah had to join them. After the Reverend Schmid prayed aloud, they went into silent meditation. Sarah mentally repeated the few prayers she had learnt by heart, but afterwards spent most of that quiet time remembering how happy she had been with the Forbeses. When they were not on their knees, her companions read aloud from their Bibles. Again Sarah had to join them; but this she enjoyed doing as the Reverend and Mrs. Schmid never failed to praise her almost faultless renditions of the chosen passages. Thirty-three days passed; then, on a Thursday morning in June, they awoke to find that during the night the *Bathurst* had dropped anchor at Sierra Leone's seaside capital, Freetown. But the journey was not yet over, for no docks existed, and they had to await the arrival of rowing boats to convey them to the shore.

It was an extensive harbour. Sarah enjoyed standing at the deck rails watching other ships at anchor, and the crowds of small boats occupied by women bringing fruits and vegetables to sell to the visiting sailors. She also enjoyed the view—in the distance, deep green, misted hills, streets climbing gently upward from the shore, several shingled rooftops, storeyed buildings here and there, and two kinds of palm trees that she recognized from her previous time in Africa—the soaring kind that produced coconuts, and the shorter variety from whose shiny red nuts women in Oke-Adan and Abomey extracted oil for cooking and making soap. From what she could see from the ship, Freetown, though much hillier, was rather like what she remembered of Badagry.

The boat-men who rowed them ashore were black; so were all the uniformed officials in the customs shed, as well as the porters standing just outside the doors, waiting to be hired. Sarah had mixed emotions about being surrounded by people with skin as dark as hers—a sense of ease that nobody thought her exotic enough to be stared at, but also a certain discomfort for, with few exceptions, her previous experiences among black people had been anything but pleasant. Eventually they emerged from the customs sheds. Among the few white people waiting outside, they saw a man in a clerical collar standing with a tall, slim woman in a pale blue dress and a broad-brimmed straw hat. The moment she noticed them, the woman broke away and strode up to Reverend and Mrs. Schmid, her right arm outstretched.

'Welcome to Freetown,' she said. 'I am Julia Sass. I hope you had a pleasant journey.'

They exchanged firm handshakes. Reverend Schmid told her that the journey had been quite enjoyable once the sea grew calmer.

'I know exactly what you mean,' she said. 'Hard going till you reach the Canary Islands…And this must be our special pupil, Sarah Bonetta.'

'Yes,' said Mrs. Schmid, looking fondly down at Sarah. 'And we are handing her over to you with the utmost regret. She was a delightful companion.'

Miss Sass looked down at Sarah with only the faintest of smiles.

'Welcome home,' she said. 'Now, thank Reverend and Mrs. Schmid for taking care of you and we'll be on our way.'

Sarah did as she was told.

The white man, obviously there to meet the Schmids, had been right behind Miss Sass. He soon led them away, followed by four muscular porters, pulling their luggage in hand carts.

'We have to walk a little way,' Miss Sass said when Sarah's trunks had been loaded onto another set of hand carts. 'No coaches here, I'm afraid. I brought an extra porter along in case you become too tired. He will carry you on his back.'

After her past experiences, the thought of being carried by a black man was enough to make Sarah hurriedly assure Miss Sass that she could walk any distance.

'Where I lived, we walked everywhere except when I was going to visit the Queen at Windsor Castle; then, we went by coach.'

Her fluent English and polished accent, as well as her casual mention of visiting Queen Victoria impressed Julia Sass far more than the information she had received from the Reverend Venn's correspondence.

'Very good,' she said, 'because we do a lot of walking here; horses don't thrive anymore...'

They had to climb a winding path to street level.

'It's not as pleasant as walking in England, though, on account of the heat and unpaved streets. Apart from loose stones and tufts of hard grass, animals and chickens roam freely about, and whenever it rains one has to watch out for puddles...'

They reached the top of the path. Across the street, and a little to the right, stood a large, rectangular, reddish brown, stone building with a tall tower.

'We are now on Water Street and that is St. George's Anglican Church. It will become a cathedral when we have a bishop, which will be soon,' said Miss Sass. 'We come here to worship on Sundays, but in the rainy season, only if the weather is fine. The rains can be extremely heavy here.'

St. George's Anglican Church reminded Sarah of England, so she was feeling acutely homesick when Miss Sass said,

'Do you remember that there are only two seasons in this part of the world?'

'No, ma'am,' she replied, without even trying to remember.

'Yes, there are only two seasons here—wet and dry. The rainy season has begun, so we are most fortunate that it hasn't rained today; otherwise our shoes would have been covered in mud by now... By the way, please call me Miss Sass.'

'Yes, Miss Sass,' Sarah said.

There were scores of other people in the wide street, all of them either coffee black or cocoa brown, some of them carrying food and other items on their heads, and in all sorts of containers. Some were dressed in adaptations of the clothes white people wore, while others had on attire similar to what Sarah had been used to seeing before being taken to England. Bony sheep, and goats, and scrawny chickens roamed about, obliging them to slow their steps from time to time. A heavy-set woman approached them. She had a basket on her head that smelled of fish, and a baby strapped to her back with a cloth.

'Ow do, ma,' she said as she walked past.

'Good Morning,' Miss Sass replied. She said to Sarah,

'Most of the people here speak a kind of broken English, mixed with other languages. I don't allow it at our school because it makes learning proper English more difficult for the girls. *You* won't have a problem, of course…'

They came to the end of Water Street, and made a right turn into a wide, upwardly sloping thoroughfare called Wilberforce Street. It crossed an even broader street, which Miss Sass told Sarah was Oxford Street. She pointed out a building on the north-eastern corner.

'That is the Church Mission House. I used to live there; and the school used to be there before we moved.'

After Oxford Street, they had to cross Westmoreland Street before coming to another section of Wilberforce Street. Then they veered left.

'We are now on Kissy Street,' said Miss Sass. Also broad, Kissy Street was quite short and in a few minutes, a change of direction to the right, brought them to another thoroughfare.

'We are now entering Kissy Road,' said Miss Sass.

Ever curious and eager to learn, Sarah asked why there were two roads with the same name, but the first one was called a street.

'That's a good question,' Miss Sass answered, pleased that Sarah had been paying attention. 'It happens in England, too, you know. I don't have an answer regarding the one we just left, but this road leads to a village further on which bears the same name. By the way,' she added, 'do you know the difference between a street and a road?'

'No, Miss Sass.'

'Usually, though not always, streets lead to other streets in a town or city, whereas roads lead to other parts of the same town or city, or to other places. Have you learnt much Geography yet?'

'No, Miss Sass.'

'Well you are going to learn a lot of Geography here. We expect our girls to know something about the world they live in.'

Sarah delighted Miss Sass further by saying with a smile in her voice, 'I shall like that. I like learning new things.'

To the right of Kissy Road, Sarah wrinkled her nose at the dank smell of decay coming from a strip of swampy, grass-covered land. She noticed several uncultivated green acres on the slope beyond it. On the opposite side of the road stood a large two-storeyed, half stone, half clapboard building with a wide verandah.

'And here we are.' said Miss Sass. 'The Female Institution.'

At last, Sarah thought with relief. Her calves had begun to ache, and her straw bonnet and light clothes no longer protected her from the broiling sun. Miss Sass had uttered no complaint, but her flushed cheeks and the damp stains at the armpits of her frock were enough to let Sarah know that she, too, must have been feeling extremely overheated. A short, brown skinned man with sunken cheeks, greeted them at the iron gate. His flat-topped cap concealed whatever hair he had.

'This is Moses,' Miss Sass told Sarah. 'The girls and the matron call him, Pa Moses. He looks after the yard, guards the gate, and does odd jobs…Moses, let one of the porters help you take the trunks upstairs.'

There were no pupils in sight when they entered the yard and, pointing to the ground floor of the building, Miss Sass explained that they were engaged in quiet reading.

'That room serves both as classroom and dining-room,' she said. 'We have a big back yard where we have the latrines and bathrooms; you'll be sharing mine. There is enough room for a well, and for the girls to keep little gardens.'

A wooden staircase took them up to the living quarters. Miss Sass had adjacent rooms—one a bedroom and the other her sitting-room. Next to her bedroom was a much smaller room which she told Sarah would be hers. Across the corridor, she showed Sarah a large room with ten low beds.

'We have eighteen pupils at present, ten of whom are boarders. This, is their dormitory...All the girls fetch their own bath water from a tank downstairs. Moses keeps it filled from the well, but as I've been told to make sure you take warm baths, I'll get him to fetch yours. Also, since you are now more used to English ways, you'll have your meals with me.' She added with a tired smile, 'I'll leave you to settle down now. Matron will be coming up soon to see you.'

Sarah removed her bonnet and sat on the bed. She looked round her room. The bed was narrow and the mattress much thinner and harder than she had become used to; but the room had a chest of drawers, a book case, and a commode and wash basin on a stand, all similar to the ones in the Forbes's home. Another pang of homesickness brought the prickle of tears, but she quickly blinked them away and jumped to her feet when a middle-aged woman entered the room, after knocking just once. Her chest reminded Sarah of a well-padded pillow, but she was quite slender from her waist down. She startled Sarah by calling her, 'Princess,' before introducing herself.

'I am Mrs. Cole, the matron. I am also the cook. The otha gals are still at their lessons, but when they finish I will send one of them up to help you unpack your trunks. Let me open them for you, then I will take you to Miss Sass. She wants you to eat with ha.'

'Thank you, ma'am; she already told me.'

'The other gals call me Mama Cole, but Miss Sass says *you* will call me, Mrs. Cole.'

Sarah wondered why she should be different, but said, 'Yes, Mrs. Cole.'

Lunch with Miss Sass consisted of English potatoes, and a beef stew, much tastier than 'Cook's' creations in Winkfield, but the side vegetable of boiled greens stirred an unpleasant memory of the kind of food she and Mahoussi used to eat in King Ghezo's court. However, it was the ripe banana they had for dessert that she found hard to swallow, the problem being that the first taste of its smooth deliciousness suddenly reminded her of her mother. It was *she* who had taught her the right way to eat a banana—to peel it as she consumed it, instead of removing all the skin beforehand.

'What's the matter, Sarah?' Miss Sass asked in some alarm,

At first Sarah said there was nothing the matter, but as Miss Sass continued to watch her with a concerned frown, she told her the truth.

Like the rest of the missionary community, Julia Sass had heard the horrific story of the raid on Oke-Adan that led to Sarah's kidnapping, and it had strengthened her deep conviction that the only way to end such barbarity among Africans was to convert them to Christianity. She put her hand over Sarah's small fingers and looked straight into her eyes.

'What happened to your family and to you was terrible, just terrible; but it has turned out for the best, hasn't it? Already you are far, far above the other girls here...You have learned what *we* consider good manners, you speak English better than many people born in England, and I have learned that you also play the piano. Most important of all, you have come to know the Lord. He must have saved your life for a reason, Sarah. *I* believe it was so you could help teach your people His ways. Only then will they stop acting so wickedly to each other.'

As usual, Sarah gave her full attention to what was being said. She realized that Miss Sass was trying to make her feel better about her past sufferings; but intelligent as she was, the idea that she had been saved from a horrible death to carry out some divine purpose was beyond her nine-year-old comprehension. And it showed. Miss Sass tried to press home her point in another way.

'Tomorrow you'll meet Abigail Crowther,' she said, 'one of our older, day pupils. Her father, was captured by slave-hunters when he was just twelve years old. Fortunately, one of our men-of-war rescued him and brought him here. He is now doing wonderful missionary work among Yorubas in Abeokuta, which I understand isn't far from your former home town...Do you know what he told someone I know? That being captured turned out to be a blessing because it introduced him to Christ and to education. He has translated the Book of Common Prayer into Yoruba, as well as some parts of the New Testament...Isn't that amazing? *He* is one example of how God brings good out of evil. You will be another, I'm sure, if you continue the way you have begun. Now, finish your banana. We can't afford to waste food.'

Sarah did as she was told, albeit still with some difficulty. She returned to her room and had begun to unpack her trunks when a girl, who seemed somewhat older than her, knocked on the door and entered.

'Good aftanoon, Princess Sarah,' she said, with a broad smile. 'My name is Rebecca...Rebecca Leigh.'

Sarah acknowledged her greeting and invited her to sit beside her on the bed. Rebecca subjected her to several moments of scrutiny before saying,

'Is it true that you are a princess?'

Sarah tilted her cheek towards her.

'Look at these marks; they show that I am a princess.'

'Oh, o,' was all Rebecca said. She had seen too many tribal marks in her village and around the town to find Sarah's particularly interesting; her hair, or the lack of it, was far more worthy of comment.

'Why is your hair short like that?' she said. 'I thought a princess will have long, long hair… like a Mami Wata.'

Sarah's brow furrowed in puzzlement.

'A Mami Wata…What's that?'

From Rebecca's description she realized that the girl was talking about a mermaid.

'Oh, you mean a mermaid,' she said.

'Mamaid is the English word for Mami Wata?' Rebecca asked.

'Yes; but even if I were a mermaid, my hair would not fall down my back. Negroes don't have hair that falls down their backs.'

'I know,' said Rebecca. 'But yours should be more long…longa, because you are a princess.…If I plant it for you it will grow…'

'Plant? What do you mean?'

Rebecca showed what she meant by making twisting movements with her fingers. Sarah could not suppress a giggle.

'Oh, you mean, plat—p-l-a-i-t, ' she said and giggled again when Rebecca said, with a look of astonishment,

'Plat is spelled p-l-a-i-t?'

She doubled up with amusement when Sarah nodded. 'This English will kill me o,' she said, and Sarah decided that she liked her.

'When can you plait my hair?' she asked.

'On Sunday afternoon—that is when we do hair; but I have to ask Mama Cole first because you are a high-up. I don't know if high-ups plant...plat their hair...Or you can ask Miss Sass.'

Another poignant memory flashed through Sarah's mind then; it was of her mother's crooning voice as she combed out the kinks in her hair, trying not to hurt her too much. She quickly changed the subject.

'Where are your shoes?' she asked, having noticed Rebecca's large bare feet. Rebeca splayed her toes.

'I don't have.'

'You don't have shoes?' Sarah remembered a time when *she* went about barefooted, but assumed that girls who attended a school called the Female Institution would all have shoes.

The church pays my school fees because my fatha and motha are poor, and there are four of us—I am the oldest,' Rebecca explained. 'My fatha is a carpenta, and my motha makes cassava bread to sell with fried bonga. She goes to the road near our house. We live in Wellington...Ova yonda; afta Kissy.' She waved vaguely towards her left.

'Oh', Sarah said, and since she could think of nothing to add, went back to removing her belongings from the trunks.

The unpacking took much longer than necessary because Rebecca had never seen so many fine things—cotton hose, frilly pantalettes, shiny coloured ribbons that slid through her fingers, soap that smelled like flowers, pretty bonnets, white bedsheets and pillowcases, soft bath towels, yards of coloured muslin, prints for frocks, aprons, and sweet smelling pomade for her hair. She exclaimed over several items, holding them up for admiration, before helping Sarah put them away. Sarah's second trunk was a treasure trove of children's books with coloured pictures, writing pads and envelopes, dozens of pencils, a game called Snakes and Ladders, another called Tiddly Winks, and another called Spillikins, boxes of water colours and blocks of paper to use with them, a small hand-held mirror, and several boxes of candles. Rebecca's eyes grew wider and wider as she went through the various items. Photographs also drew her attention. Sarah pointed to a large one in a bronze frame embossed with flowers.

'That is the Queen of England. *She* sent me here.'

'*She* sent you here?'

Rebecca sat back on the bed to take a closer look.

Having remarked on the Queen's surprising lack of physical beauty, she said, 'Miss Sass dresses just like her; even her hair.'

'That's how English women dress,' said Sarah who had joined her on the bed. 'The queen has more petticoats under her skirts because it is cold over there, and her frocks are more beautiful because she is rich; very, very rich. You should see her house.'

'And *she* sent you here. You are lucky o.' Rebecca said, but as if she fully accepted her station in life, her voice held not the slightest hint of envy.

Eventually, the girls made up the bed and went down to inform Mrs. Cole that the work was done. She summoned Pa Moses to take the empty trunks to the common box-room, then said to Rebecca,

'Leave Princess Sarah to rest now. You will meet again tomorrow.'

Sarah was glad to be released for she was wilting from the heat, that long walk, the exertion of unpacking her trunks, and her first encounter with her new school mate. Back in her room she picked up a book and absently began flicking through the pages; but the daylight faded all at once and thunder rumbled overhead in an alarming way. She quickly dived into bed and covered her head with her pillow. In no time she was so sound asleep that she never heard the rain pounding the roof. Miss Sass decided not to wake her for tea, but roused her for supper.

Over that meal, Sarah asked if Rebecca Leigh could plait her hair to make it grow faster.

'I suppose so,' Miss Sass said without enthusiasm. 'And when it's long enough, you'll be able to do it up in neat folds so that you look a bit older, and less like a native. In which case, I might even ask you to help teach some of the girls to speak better English.'

Sarah had enjoyed helping Lucy Forbes with her lessons and teaching Rebecca Leigh new words.

'I would like that,' she said, beaming.

Later, Miss Sass said, 'I know you had a long nap this afternoon, but get back to bed as soon as you can. You've had quite a hectic day and we don't want you falling ill now, do we? Matron normally rings a bell when it's time to blow out candles, but I expect you to be asleep long before then. She also rings a bell when it's time to get up in the morning... Oh, one last thing before you go...' she added, as Sarah began to leave the table, 'our timetable.'

She went on to describe the school's daily routine which, Sarah discovered, was not unlike what she had become used to with the Forbeses, except that the day began at 6 o'clock, and the first three hours after breakfast were devoted to deepening the girls' knowledge of Christianity. They learned formal prayers from the Book of Common Prayer, learned and practised simple new hymns, and studied those parts of the Bible Miss Sass considered most important for their religious and moral education.

'Do you know the Doxology, Sarah, Praise God from whom all blessings flow?'

'Yes, Miss Sass,' Sarah said, and sang the first line.

'That's it. And I must say, you have a *lovely* voice. I can see that you are going to be an asset to the school. Off you go, then...And don't forget to say your prayers.'

CHAPTER NINE
Settling Down

Excited fidgeting greeted Miss Sass when she appeared with Sarah the next morning, for most of the girls had never met someone more or less their age, and who looked like them, but who wore expensive-looking shoes, hose and a pretty dress that fitted her perfectly. Their eyes shone with curiosity as Miss Sass introduced them to, 'Princess Sarah', who felt almost as awkward as she had felt the first time the Forbeses took her to the village church at Winkfield. She was glad when the introductions were over and Miss Sass directed her to an empty chair.

She went to the blackboard, wrote the first verse of the hymn they would learn that day, and then to Sarah's dismay, said,

'Princess Sarah will read it out, and you will learn it line by line as usual before I teach you the tune.'

She handed Sarah a paper with the hymn written out on it, and told her to carry on. Sarah was confident about reading aloud, but her knees still felt wobbly as she rose to her feet and faced the class.

'Do no sinful action,

Speak no angry word,'

That was as far as she read before she heard a titter. She gave Miss Sass an uncertain look. Miss Sass pursed her lips but told her to continue.

'You belong to Jesus,'

Children of the Lord.'

More titters spluttered from among the girls till it seemed that most of them were stifling laughter. Unaccustomed to being the object of ridicule, Sarah stopped reading again and, on the verge of tears, started folding up the paper. Miss Sass sprang to her feet, her cheeks flushed with anger.

'You may go back to your seat now,' she told Sarah with deceptive calmness. As Sarah complied, she yelled at the rest of the girls, 'Stand up.' Levelling an even angrier gaze at the laggards, she raised her voice another decibel. 'At once.'

Her severity quickly restored decorum.

'You should be thoroughly ashamed of yourselves,' she scolded, 'especially to a new girl, and one of her standing. I asked Princess Sarah to read out the hymn because I wanted you to realize that an African like yourselves could learn to speak English well. It was for your benefit; but instead of listening and learning, you sat there giggling like a bunch of idiots...You will remain standing until you have learned the hymn.'

She glowered at them for a moment longer before going back to her desk from which she took them through the verses line by line. Only when she was satisfied that everyone knew the words by heart did she go to the harmonium near her desk and start playing the tune. Sarah could never resist music. She stood up herself and joined the singing lesson, which might explain why, when the session ended and Miss Sass went for her short tea break, some of the older girls came up to her, said they were sorry and started conversations.

In Miss Sass's absence, the girls divided the room into two classes, using a wide lattice screen, and on her return she gave them lessons in Arithmetic, followed by English grammar and Geography; half of them did written work, while she imparted fresh knowledge to the other half. One hour later, an elderly African woman entered the classroom to take over. She taught and supervised handwork and was carrying a colourful basket. She cut an impressive figure in an ankle-length, long-sleeved cotton dress, with frills at the wrists and close to the hem, and a belt tied loosely at the waist. The dress was a pale mauve, with bunches of white grapes printed over it at regular intervals. A cotton head wrap in the same colours, but with a geometric pattern, hid her hair. Her brightly patterned footwear caught Sarah's eye.

'Good morning, girls,' she said in the confident tone of a woman who knows she is well dressed.

'Good morning, Mrs. Dixon,' the girls chorused, which was how Sarah learned her name.

'I see a new face,' Mrs. Dixon said.

'Yes, ma. She is Princess Sarah,' one of the girls piped up. 'She came from England.'

'*Hmm*,' said Mrs. Dixon. Already briefed by Mrs. Cole, she was only feigning surprise.

'Welcome, Princess Sarah,' she said. 'Pleased to meet you. Today I am going to teach marking.'

She showed them the materials they would be working with: big blunt needles, brightly coloured yarns and pieces of open weave canvas. In practice, marking turned out to be no different from the needlepoint embroidery that had been Mary Forbes's hobby. Sarah loved it from the start; and when she learned that the tops of Mrs. Dixon's shoes were the finished product, was determined to become expert enough to give some of her own handiwork away as presents.

Miss Sass returned to supervise an hour of reading practice before lunch for which, as expected, Sarah joined her. They had a ripe mango for dessert and were finishing the succulent slices, when she said to Sarah,

'I hope those silly girls didn't upset you too much; they behave so badly sometimes.'

'They did a little,' Sarah confessed, 'but during the break some of them came and said they were sorry.'

'I'm very glad to hear that,' Miss Sass said, and for the first time in Sarah's presence, smiled widely enough to show her teeth. 'When such things happen, and they are bound to from time to time, just remember that very few of these girls have had the privilege of the kind of home you had with your guardians in England.'

'That is what Captain Forbes said when some street boys in London called me names; that they had no one to teach them good manners.'

'And he was right; but in this world there are also people who are unkind, even cruel in their ways. You'll have to get used to them, as well, and not take what they say or do too much to heart. Just keep on doing your best and praying that they will come to know the Lord…Now run along; I'm expecting people from the mission office any time now. They are coming to have a look at that acre of open ground across the road. I have suggested to the mission that they acquire it to put up a proper building for the school so it no longer has to keep moving. It started in a village up in the hills, you know; then, as more pupils came, it moved to the Church Mission House, and then to this building. Each time, we've quickly run out of space. This house will soon become too small.'

She looked pale and tired after the exertions and vexations of the morning, and even more so when Sarah joined her for supper that evening. After scarcely touching her food, she said,

'I feel a fever coming on, and shall have to stay in bed over the weekend. I'm afraid you'll have to have your meals with the girls until I feel better. Hope you don't mind.'

'Oh, no, Miss Sass,' Sarah said, 'I don't mind at all.'

In fact, she was delighted that she would have an opportunity to mix with the other boarders outside the classroom.

'Rebecca Leigh says that after washing their clothes on Saturday mornings they do gardening. May I join them?'

'I don't think Her Majesty would approve of your engaging in any pursuit that will dirty your hands and roughen your palms. She wants you to grow up to be a lady.'

'But Mrs. Forbes is a lady, and *she* did gardening, ' Sarah pointed out in a small, sad voice.

'Not with her bare hands, I'm sure.'

Sarah's dejected expression made Miss Sass say, 'Tell you what, I'll write to Lady Phipps and ask her to send you some gardening gloves by the next mailing steamer. How does that sound?'

Sarah's face brightened immediately.

'And when you write to Her Majesty, as you must no later than this Sunday after church, tell her you would love to garden but don't have the proper gloves. With any luck, in a couple of months you'll be able to join the other girls.'

Sarah almost skipped away, but a few hours later, Mrs. Cole killed her joy by coming to her room with a large glass bottle containing an opaque white liquid, and insisting that she take a tablespoonful of the mixture. It tasted so vile that Sarah gagged, grimacing. Mrs Cole said, 'Mist. Alba, Princess Sarah. It is a porge.'

'Do I have to take it often?'

'Yes; every Friday evening. A good clear out to keep you healthy.'

As she prepared for bed, the prospect of a weekly dose of the nasty stuff dampened Sarah's spirits further; but the purgative served its purpose the next morning and, feeling none the worse for the experience, she enjoyed sharing with the other boarders, the simple breakfast of bread, a boiled egg, and sweet tea with goat's milk. Afterwards, she wrote her letter to the Queen, then contented herself with watching while the girls did their laundry and tended their small garden plots. The scene took her mind back to Oke-Adan and Abomey, where every household had a garden to keep its residents supplied with hot peppers, cherry tomatoes and leafy vegetables; but strangely enough, the memory caused her no pain, nor did their tasty lunch of green leaves and smoked fish, cooked in palm oil, and eaten with boiled rice. Since there was no work to be done after lunch, Mrs. Cole, who supervised meals, allowed the girls to ask her questions about England while they ate. The conversation gave her such a sense of belonging that she began to feel that she might enjoy being at the Female Institution after all.

It poured again that night, but for the puddles Miss Sass had mentioned before, no one seeing the unclouded skies and brilliant sunshine the next morning would have guessed that rain had drenched the town just a few hours earlier. After breakfast, everyone at the Female Institution walked to St. George's Church, except for Miss Sass and Pa Moses. He had Sundays off and preferred to attend church in his village. Sarah's eyes widened with astonishment at the number of well-to-do Africans in the congregation. Gloves, muslin, silk, layers of petticoats and fancy bonnets were much in evidence; even feather boas. Some of the men looked elegant in tailcoats, but others reminded her of the paunchy Sir Charles Phipps, which forced her to suppress giggles.

Four hours later, the boarders sat down to lunch, the basics of which Mrs. Cole had prepared the evening before—a rich beef stew, on a bed of rice cooked in tomato sauce, with boiled cabbage as a vegetable. On this occasion, Sarah experienced no difficulty eating a banana afterwards. Having her hair done was a greater trial for, as Rebecca's fingers moved over her head oiling and parting, combing and weaving, a memory of her mother pierced her heart again.

Rebecca noticed Sarah flicking away tears and stopped what she was doing.

'Is it so painful?' she asked in surprise,

'Not the plaiting. My mother used to do my hair; that's why I'm sad. She is dead…'

'Oh. Please accept my sympathy,' Rebecca said, showing it in her eyes and voice. 'What happened?'

Sarah told her what she remembered of the raid on Oke-Adan and its aftermath. It was not much, but enough to make Rebecca catch her breath in open-mouthed horror.

'So, how did you reach England?' she asked.

Sarah told her the rest of the story up to the Queen's decision to send her to Freetown.

Once again, Rebecca said, 'You are lucky o.' But this time she went on in a regretful tone, 'Our people can be bad…very wicked. Black people, hunting for slaves, caught my fatha and motha—from different towns. A man-of-war rescued them when the ship was taking them to Brazil.'

'Brazil? Where is that?'

'I don't know; some far place. It was the man-of-war that brought them here… We are Igbo. How about you?'

'Yoruba. My real name is Aina. It means that I was born with my cord around my neck…My mother told me that.

Rebecca stopped in the middle of a plait.

'You were born with your cord around your neck and you did not die?… God is wonderful o,' she sighed, and resumed her work.

'Do you have an Igbo name?' Sarah asked.

'Yes, Ndidi.'

'Ndidi. It's a nice name.'

'It means Patience.'

The hair plaiting continued in silence. Finally, Rebecca sat back and, after a moment, declared herself satisfied with the result.

'It fits your face, and your nice round head.'

Sarah patted the plaits. Her head felt strangely light and she could hardly wait to see herself in the mirror. In her room, she turned this way and that, undecided as to whether she liked the way she looked.

Miss Sass gave her own verdict when they met at breakfast the next morning. She seemed in better health than the last time they ate together, but was not in the best of moods and gave her verdict on Sarah's hair after giving her scarcely a look.

'It'll do for now; let's just hope it does grow fast.'

The meal went on in silence till, to make conversation, Sarah asked whether the mission had agreed to buy the land.

Miss Sass looked even more depressed.

'No; they say they'll need to raise the money first; the government won't help…The only good news is that they are sure the government will agree to reserve the land for the school.'

'I'm sorry,' Sarah murmured.

'There is some *really* good news, though. When we knew you were coming, and were learning to play the piano, I asked the mission to provide one for the school. Besides, I find playing that harmonium quite a strain. The piano is arriving on the next mail steamer, *and* with music books.'

The glad light in Sarah's eyes gave Miss Sass a reason to be cheerful, and she smiled.

CHAPTER TEN
The Star Pupil

Before the end of her first July in Freetown, Sarah went down with a one of her feverish colds and coughs. It was the first of several she would contract during that rainy season and in the early months of the new year when the dry, dusty Harmattan winds blew in from the Sahara Desert; but when her strength returned, her brilliance dazzled both staff and pupils. By the start of 1852, she had taken over playing the hymns at their daily religious sessions, and was so far ahead of the other girls in all her classes that Miss Sass decided to introduce her to French. Her classmates sought her help with English grammar and pronunciation, and with arithmetic, which she gave with such kindness, that some of them asked her to become their adopted sister. She should have been content, or as content as she could ever be away from England and the people she considered family. Instead, as the months went by she grew more and more dissatisfied.

It had something to do with her uneasiness about her special privileges—her private room when the other girls slept in a dormitory, her warm baths when the others had to use cold water even on chilly rainy season or Harmattan mornings; not having to do any chores; Miss Sass taking her on delightful excursions to the quaint mountain villages and pristine, sandy beaches, while the other boarders remained confined to the school except for the weekly outing to church and back. And she disliked being singled out for attention and praise whenever missionaries and other visitors came to see the school, which was fairly often. One May morning, Miss Sass said over breakfast,

'Last night I had a bright idea to do with Her Majesty's birthday on the twenty-fourth. It's time the girls learned our national anthem. I think we could use the occasion to teach it to them, as well as honour the Queen. My idea is that you invite all the girls to tea—after school, since it falls on a Monday. Mrs. Cole will organize tea and cakes. After tea, you will play and sing the national anthem, which I know you've mastered; then you'll teach it to them.'

'But they will think I am showing off,' Sarah protested.

'Nonsense. You are of an entirely different class from the other girls, and they know it.'

That was the moment Sarah realized exactly what had been troubling her. It was the way Miss Sass stressed her difference from the other girls when, with the possible exception of her warm baths, she would gladly have given up her privileges to be just one of them. Even with the Queen taking her under her wing, she had felt she belonged when she lived with the Forbeses, and she had begun to feel she belonged during the weekend Miss Sass fell ill.

However, with obedience bred in her bones, she carried out Miss Sass's wishes. It helped that the programme included her favourite occupations—playing the piano, singing, and teaching. In the event, she enjoyed herself, as did the other girls. They always found her head and shoulder movements at the piano hilarious, and in Miss Sass's absence, felt free to giggle. But their amusement was without malice, for the most part. The words and tune of the British National Anthem were easy to learn, and they were well fortified by thick slices of Mrs. Cole's delicious cake, so hardly any time passed before they were all standing at attention before Sarah's photograph of Queen Victoria and, to her accompaniment, singing at the tops of their voices:

'God save our gracious Queen,
Long live our noble Queen,
God save the Queen!
Send her victorious,
Happy and glorious,
Long to reign over us,
God save the Queen!'

At that point, listening in her sitting-room and feeling pleased, Miss Sass deemed it time to break up the party. She joined them, just moments later, clapping, but saying, 'Well done, girls!' with an air of finality.

She praised Sarah personally when they met for supper, and Sarah had to admit that the tea party had been a good idea. Still, when they parted, she wished she were going to join the other girls in the dormitory instead of to her lonely room.

Her inner resistance to being treated differently increased as time went by, yet she was helpless to change the situation, given Miss Sass's rigid ideas about what the Queen would disapprove of, or what was appropriate for 'Princess Sarah', a title that held no meaning for her. To console herself, she practised on the piano as often as she could and did a lot of marking, using yarns and needlepoint canvas the Queen had sent at her request. Tending the garden plot she shared with Rebecca Leigh also lifted her spirits, as did their conversations during hair plaiting sessions on Sundays.

'Have you started yet?' Rebecca asked towards the end of her second year at the school .

'Started what?' Sarah asked, mystified.

'To see blood.'

'To see blood? I don't understand.'

'So, you don't know.'

'Know what?'

In frustration Sarah held on to Rebecca's wrists to stop her working, and repeated, 'Know what?'

'What happens to girls when they reach our age.'

'No. What happens?'

'When girls reach our age, blood comes out of that place every month.' she said, pointing to Sarah's lap.

Since no one had ever mentioned that part of her body in those terms, it took Sarah a moment to understand what Rebecca was talking about in that mysterious way.

'It happens to everybody?' she said as realization dawned.

'Everybody.'

'Oh, my! What should I do when it happens to me?'

'You have to put cloths there, otherwise you will stain your clothes; big white cloths, like men's handkachiefs only, thick. Let the Queen send some for you—at least one dozen. Then when it starts, tell Mama Cole. She will tell you what to do.'

'Oh, my!' Sarah said again.

Sarah waited till after supper to introduce the distasteful subject.

'Miss Sass, Rebecca Leigh says I should ask the Queen to send me some white cloths.'

For the first time in their acquaintance, Miss Sass avoided her eyes as she answered.

'Ah, yes; I should have thought of that myself, especially since we've only guessed your age. But we won't bother the Queen. Mrs. Cole can get you something suitable right here, and the sooner the better.'

'But could you please tell me more about it? Rebecca did not know why it happens.'

'Well,' Miss Sass began, 'It's something all girls have to put up with once they reach a certain age …' She paused, as if wondering how best to proceed, then gave up, saying, 'I'll write something down for you.'

Which she did, but with so little detail that Sarah remained almost as much in the dark as before. However, she was grateful to have been warned, for when nature took its course during her third year at the school, it caused her no anxiety, though it did cause her some cramping pain. Mrs. Cole gave her a dose of a linctus that tasted suspiciously like what she provided to soothe coughs, but it relieved her discomfort.

That year, ill-heath disrupted Miss Sass's meal arrangements with Sarah many times. She often could not take her classes either, so that another missionary, a Miss Wilkinson, had to come in daily to assist her. Eventually, the mission committee decided that Miss Sass needed to return to England for an indefinite period of sick leave. Miss Wilkinson took up residence in her rooms, but readily agreed when Sarah asked if she could continue eating her meals with the other boarders. Miss Wilkerson brought in another change. Sarah would continue to enjoy warm baths in solitude, but no longer in the Superintendent's private cubicle.

CHAPTER ELEVEN
The Crisis

It was one thing to answer the call to preach the Gospel to the heathen, but quite another to be capable of dealing with the challenges of running a school. Miss Wilkinson was no Miss Sass, neither was Mrs. Dicker, a missionary's wife, who was later put in charge of the Female Institution. They laid great emphasis on religious studies to the neglect of the other subjects. That soon bored the brighter girls, Sarah, among them. Boredom gave rise to unruly behaviour, which had greatly decreased under Miss Sass. The incidents of indiscipline among the girls caused frequent clashes with Miss Wilkinson and Mrs. Dicker, so that for months the general atmosphere in the school remained unhappy and tense. Sarah's bouts of illness increased. She was confined to her room and, for fear that she might spread infection, allowed no visitors except for Mrs. Cole, who brought her medication and saw to her comfort. One morning she heard wailing coming from the dormitory, but did not discover its cause till Mrs. Cole arrived.

'Your friend Rebecca had to go home today. She is not coming back…'

'Not coming back?' Sarah said in dismay. 'Was it Rebecca who was crying in the dormitory?'

'Yes. Ha fatha sent a message that ha motha put to bed yesterday, but she and the baby perished. Rebecca has gone for the burying and she will have to stay to look afta ha brotha and sistas.'

Tears rolled down Sarah's cheeks.

'I won't see her ever again?'

'She will come for ha things, Princess Sarah; you will see ha then.'

I can't stay here without Rebecca, Sarah thought when Mrs Cole left her. I *can't* stay here. Her hair had grown long enough to be arranged in neat folds with small combs, but she and Rebecca still spent hours together in the garden on Saturdays, and on Sunday afternoons. Since Miss Sass's departure, their friendship was the one thing that made her life at the Female Institution more than merely tolerable, and now even that consolation was being taken from her. She sobbed her heart out, then sat up, dried her eyes, and poured out her misery in a letter to Lady Phipps.

******

'I don't understand this,' said Miss Wilkinson some weeks later, referring to a letter she had just read. 'It's from Lady Phipps.'

'Let me see,' said Miss Sass. She had only recently returned from her sick leave and had not yet completely taken over her duties.

'I don't understand it, either,' she said after a quick read. 'The child was sent here because Her Majesty thought the climate would be better for her health? How could she now be commanding us to send her back; *and* without delay. She doesn't even ask our opinion.'

'Exactly. Sarah must have written to complain about something. She'll never admit it, though. In spite of her veneer of Englishness, I'm sure she's as African as can be when it comes to such matters. They are such evasive people, or else they tell you what they think you want to hear.'

'That may be so; but I still want to hear what she has to say. Let's call her in.'

139

Sarah could not hide her glee when, having summoned her to the sitting-room, Miss Sass informed her that, at Her Majesty's command, she would be returning to England as soon as it could be arranged.

'Were you expecting this, Sarah?'

'No, Miss Sass, but I was praying for it.'

'Did you make a complaint to Her Majesty about the school?' Miss Wilkinson wanted to know.

'I only told her the truth, Miss Wilkerson; that I am not learning much anymore, that I get coughs and colds as often as I did in England, and that I don't feel I shall ever belong here.'

'I see,' said Miss Sass. 'Well, there is no point trying to persuade you to change your mind if Her Majesty has made up hers. Reverend and Mrs. Dicker will be traveling back to England shortly. We shall arrange for them to take you along.'

If Sarah had any doubts about letting the Queen know exactly how she felt, they were dispelled when, alone in a bath cubicle some days later, she overheard one girl say to the person sharing hers, 'Let her go. Just because she talks in her nose, she thinks she is better than us. And who made her a princess? She's blacker than you and me.'

In spite of her special privileges, Sarah had never boasted or put on airs. She therefore bristled with indignation at the unfairness of the comment; but she also wiped away a tear.

The steamer sailed on the twenty-third of June. Since it was a Saturday, Miss Sass allowed a few of the older girls to accompany herself and Miss Wilkinson to the Government Wharf to bid farewell to Sarah and the Dickers. On board the steamer, Sarah looked back at the hilly streets, palm trees, and shingled roofs of Freetown, and hoped she would never see them again.

PART FIVE
Transition

CHAPTER TWELVE
A Special Friend

Palm Cottage,
Canterbury Road,
Gillingham,
Kent.
20th, August, 1855.

'Dear Miss Sass,

This is to let you know that I arrived safely. My voyage back to England was similar to the one that brought me to Sierra Leone, except that the seas remained fairly calm throughout.

Reverend and Mrs. Dicker had to take me to the CMS offices at Waterloo Street to find out where I was to stay and, as the journey from the docks to London took a long time, we did not arrive until late. We therefore spent the night in guest rooms at the mission house. My previous guardian, Mrs. Mary Forbes, who is now a widow, has moved to Scotland with her children, so Her Majesty had to make a new arrangement for me. I am now living at the above address with

Reverend and Mrs. Schoen and their family. You might know, or have heard of Reverend Schoen since he used to be a missionary in West Africa. He worked with Reverend Samuel Crowther, but became too ill to stay. They have seven children, three born in Freetown, I was surprised to learn, all now being schooled at home. A governess comes in every day to teach us.

Everyone has been very kind to me, especially Mrs. Schoen. She has told me to call her, Mama, which I find very easy to do. I only see Reverend Schoen at family prayers, which we have before breakfast. Every day he goes to Melville Hospital nearby to pray with the wounded soldiers. Mama says Britain is fighting a war in the Crimea. Thanks to your Geography lessons, I was able to find it on the map on the class-room wall. When Reverend Schoen is at home, he stays in his study. Mama says he is studying some African languages and has written books about them.

Palm Cottage is on a hill in the middle of nowhere, but I like the views of the green fields around, and prefer the quietness to being in London, which I found too noisy and crowded. I don't think I shall ever grow to like London; it's much too hectic for me.

I have not yet seen the Queen as I must await an invitation, but I expect it to be soon. Mama says that she is in London at present—at St. James's Palace.

I hope you continue to be in good health. Please give my regards to Miss. Wilkinson, Mrs. Cole and Mrs. Dixon.

Yours sincerely,
Sarah Forbes Bonetta.

Palm Cottage,
Canterbury Road,
Gillingham,
Kent.
6th January 1856.

Dear Miss Sass,

Thank you for your letter, and best wishes for the new year. I was glad to read that the land for the school has now been purchased, and the plans drawn up. I shall keep praying that the money for the building comes soon.

The Queen sent for me last month; Mama Schoen went with me. It was my first time on a train. The journey took about one hour and was much more pleasant than travelling by coach— very noisy, but much steadier. St James's Palace is enormous, but not half as grand as Windsor Castle. The Queen looked just the same, but she said she hardly recognized me. She said, 'You are so grown, Sarah, and so beautifully slender.' She also said I should teach her daughter, Alice, who is my friend, to stand as straight as I do. How can I do that when it comes naturally to me? I took some of my work books with me as she likes to see them. She said she was very pleased with my progress and asked if I was warm enough, which I thought very kind of her. I did not tell her that I had just recovered from another bad cough.

I hope the teacher who has replaced Miss Wilkinson will be of great help to you.

With affection,
Sarah F. Bonetta.

Palm Cottage,
Canterbury Road,
Gillingham, Kent.
1st July, 1856.

Dear Miss Sass,

Thank you for your last letter. We are having a break from lessons for the summer and the Queen and Lady Phipps, planned a couple of visits for me—first to Windsor Castle, then up to Scotland to visit the Forbeses. They were the first family to give me a home in England and I had thought I would never see them again. It was a very long and tiring journey up to Scotland, but worth it. I was delighted to see the Forbeses again. They, too, seemed very glad to see me. Mrs. Forbes introduced me to the rest of her family.

I was nervous about going by myself from Gillingham to Windsor, but Mama put the conductor in charge of me and Lady Phipps met me at the station with the pony cart, so it was all right. I have grown to like Lady Phipps very much and was glad to have her all to myself. Her husband and children had gone to Norfolk. She, too, has asked me to call her, Mama, so I now have two English mothers! I saw the Queen the next day.

I am so glad that I learned to mark. I made a pair of slippers as a present for Prince Albert. The Queen liked them so much, that she asked me to make her a pair. Please let Mrs. Dixon know; I'm sure she will be pleased.

I have discovered novels, though Mama Schoen only allows me to read those she approves of. She says not all novels are suitable for Christians to read. So far my favourites are Pride and Prejudice, Emma and Persuasion by Jane Austen, and some of the books Charles Dickens has published so far. Among those, my favourites are David Copperfield, Oliver Twist and A Christmas Carol. Mama Schoen insists that I spend twice as much time reading my Bible as I spend reading novels. Fortunately I also enjoy doing that, so it is no hardship.

Yours affectionately,
Sarah Bonetta.

Palm Cottage,
Canterbury Road,
Gillingham,
Kent.
1st March, 1858.

Dear Miss Sass,

What good news that the mission has received an unexpected gift of money from a Reverend and Mrs. Walsh, so that you can now start working on the new building for the Female Institution. I was very sad to learn that they lost their young daughter, Annie, who had wanted to become a missionary, but remembered your telling me that, by God's grace, good can come out of terrible events. I pray that He is comforting her parents.

Life has been exciting lately. First of all, the Princess Royal, the Queen's oldest daughter, also called Victoria, married Prince Frederick William of Prussia on January twenty-fifth. The Queen commanded my presence at the ceremony and even sent me the clothes I should wear. They were absolutely beautiful. Before the wedding, Mama Schoen took us all to see the festive decorations in central London which were wonderful to behold. There were hundreds of guests at the wedding, most of them royalty from all over Europe. Princess Victoria's bridal dress was like something out of a fairytale. Her bouquet had orange flowers trimmed with myrtle. The same flowers trimmed her veil. Princess Alice and her sisters were bridesmaids. They also wore lovely dresses—white lace over satin, trimmed with corn flowers and daisies, with a wreath of the same flowers over their heads. All her brothers wore kilts. They looked splendid.

Mama Schoen's daughter, Harriet, married a missionary not long afterwards, and I was a bridesmaid. It was nothing like the royal wedding, but they seemed much more fond of each other than Princess Victoria and her husband. I'm not sure where they will be sent to do their missionary work.

Affectionately,
Sarah Forbes Bonetta.

Palm Cottage,
Canterbury Road,
Gillingham,
Kent.
8th December, 1860.

Dear Miss Sass,

I doubt that you will receive this before Christmas, so I shall send you my best wishes for the new year.

Now that my formal schooling is over, I travel around a fair bit, visiting friends of Mama Schoen, who have taken a liking to me. As a result, I almost suffered a huge embarrassment recently. I went straight from one visit to Windsor Castle, only to discover that the Queen's cousin had died and everyone was in mourning—the women in deep black and the men with black arm bands. Fortunately, I stay in Lady Phipps's apartment at the castle and the Queen never sends for me as soon as I arrive. Still, what a scramble it was to get my one good black dress sent from Gillingham to Windsor in time. It would have been a dreadful faux pas to appear before Her Majesty in coloured clothes.

Princess Alice recently became engaged to Prince Louis of Hesse-Darmstadt (another German), though she is only seventeen. Arranged marriages seem to be the custom among European royal families. I don't think I would like that at all.

Affectionately,
Sarah Bonetta.

--

Windsor Castle,
5th August, 1861.

Dear Miss Sass,

I was delighted to receive your letter telling me that the foundation stone for the new school building has at last been laid. I pray that the work goes on without a hitch and that you do not find the supervision of it too taxing. Laying a broad walk of gravel across that swamp and all the way up the slope sounded like a huge endeavour, even if you did not undertake the labour yourself.

Yes, I do sometimes miss the sights and sounds of Freetown, especially, women with babies on their backs, the muslim call to prayers, cocks crowing in the mornings, and the different palm trees. Their leaves make such pretty patterns against the sky, especially when it is blue. And I also miss the red rice and beef stew Mrs. Cole made for our Sunday lunches; but on the whole I prefer to be in England. I am very happy here.

I have thought about the question you asked in your last letter: whether I would consider becoming a missionary. My honest answer is that, much as I love the Lord, I don't think I have the calling, or the stamina for a life of hardship and deprivation. I know you've had hopes of me following in your footsteps, but please don't be too disappointed. I have to be true to myself, even though becoming a missionary would solve a problem I have. With Princess Alice's engagement, Mama Phipps has told me that the Queen is talking about the need to find me a suitable husband. As I mentioned in another letter, I hate the thought of an arranged marriage.

In this regard, please, please remember me in your prayers.

Always with affection,
Sarah Forbes Bonetta.

CHAPTER THIRTEEN
The Queen's Displeasure

What Sarah did not tell Miss Sass was that she had already received a proposal of marriage from a Mr. James Pinson Labulo Davies. She was sure that Lady Phipps, Mrs. Schoen, and the Reverend Venn had all had a hand in it; otherwise how did Mr. Davies know where to find her? He introduced himself in a letter, which included a small photograph, and nothing in his image or in the letter inclined her even to consider the proposal. She looked at the picture, reread the letter, looked at the image again and her mind said, no. Not a widower, thirteen years older than her, apparently on the short side, and who looked unpolished, despite his fine three-piece suit and watch chain. Not that she hoped to marry an Englishman, but her eighteen-year-old mind dreamt of an African version of Mr. Darcy and other aristocratic characters in novels she had read—tall and noble in appearance, whereas Mr. Davies could only be described as very ordinary. She tried to imagine his arms around her and shuddered. In his favour, Mr. Davies expressed himself well, and had become wealthy from commercial shipping and other business ventures. He was certainly in a position to provide for her in a manner even better than that to which she had grown accustomed; but then she would have to live mostly in Africa. No, her mind said again; a thousand times no.

'Well?' Mrs. Schoen asked with a hopeful lift to her voice.

'I have written to reject his proposal, Mama. I can't marry a man I don't love, and I can never love Mr. Davies.'

'How do you know that, Sally? Reverend Venn knows him very well and vouches for his good character. At least, agree to meet him. Give him a chance.'

Sarah's response to her guardian's plea was a resolute shake of her head.

Oh, dear, thought Mrs. Schoen with a sigh. The young man sounded so suitable.

'I have to respond to Lady Phipps's letter,' she said and hurried away.

A few days later, Sarah was in Lady Phipps's apartment at Windsor Castle.

'Sally', she said, 'As you know, Her Majesty is very fond of you. So is Mrs. Schoen and so am I; but your stubborn attitude just won't do.'

'I can't marry a man I don't love, Mama, and I can't love Mr. Davies. I would be miserable, and so would he. He deserves a happy marriage; especially after losing his first wife so early.'

Despite her fondness for Sarah, Lady Phipps realized that the situation required more than gentle persuasion.

'So what is to become of you then? Don't expect Her Majesty to foot your bills forever; before you know it you'll be twenty-one and on your own.'

Sarah had never before heard that sharp tone coming from Lady Phipps, and it gave her pause. Lady Phipps noticed her uncertainty and seized the advantage.

'In this country, upper class women without money of their own have only two choices: they either become private governesses, or companions to elderly ladies. I doubt that a position as a private governess would be open to an African woman here, even if you wanted one. A companion to some elderly woman, perhaps, though even that is doubtful. And, with your intelligence, you would be bored to tears in no time. *Then* what would you do? There would have been no problem had you chosen to become a missionary, but Mrs. Schoen tells me that is not an option you are willing to consider…'

'The right man will come along, Mama,' Sarah murmured.

'From where, may I ask, and when? I imagine that Africans of Mr. Davies's calibre are few and far between. No, my girl. For your own good, you need to go to your room, think long and hard about your future, and come to the right conclusion.

However, Sarah's conclusion was not what Lady Phipps wanted to hear. Like Mrs. Schoen, she said,

'At least, agree to meet him.' But Sarah replied, 'What would be the use of that, Mama, when I have already made up my mind?'

'Very well then,' Lady Phipps said briskly. 'I shall tell Her Majesty how things stand. But let me warn you; she is going to be most displeased.'

There was no further discussion on the subject. Sarah returned to Gillingham that very day.

The Queen's response reached her through a letter from Lady Phipps to Mrs. Schoen who, knowing how happy Sarah had been at Palm Cottage, gave her the news with apprehension.

'Sally, this makes us very sad, but Her Majesty believes a change of residence would help you take a more realistic view of your situation.'

Even before hearing the details of the new arrangement, Sarah's eyes stung with tears at the thought of once again being separated, at the Queen's command, from people and places she had grown to love.

Close to tears herself, Mrs. Schoen went on, 'She has decided to send you to stay with one of Lady Phipps's in-laws, and for an indefinite period. The woman lives in Brighton.'

'So I am to be punished.' It was not a question but a sullen statement.

'Don't think of it, that way, Sally.'

'How else can I think of it, Mama?' Sarah said, her voice cracking with the pain of it. 'Her Majesty is punishing me for not falling in line with her wishes. Is Mr. Davies's wealth all that matters?'

Mrs. Schoen could think of nothing more comforting to say than, 'We shall be praying for you, Sally.'

'Will your prayers bring me a man I could love?'

She felt no less bitter when she entered her new home. Its inmates were elderly: Miss Sophia Welsh, who was Lady Phipps's sister-in-law, her own widowed sister, and their nephew. The only young people were the two maids; and with its tiny, musty rooms and shabby furnishings, the house itself, at 17 Clifton Hill, did nothing to lift her spirits. It overlooked the waters of the English Channel, but that one redeeming feature she could not enjoy in the second back bedroom that was hers. How can I stay in this dreary place, she thought in despair, and among people with whom I have nothing in common and who, while very polite, can't hide their discomfort at having a black person in their midst? It was punishment indeed, but for several months that did nothing to concentrate her mind on solving the problem of her future. Instead, wallowing in self-pity, she mainly kept to herself, praying for guidance which did not come, doing her marking, and speaking only when spoken to. Inevitably, she went down with a cold and cough, which forced her to remain in bed for more than a week.

It was the kindness of her hostess and her relations when she fell ill that began to melt her resistance to her present circumstances. The ladies came up to her room every day to ask how she was feeling, and suggested ways to make her more comfortable, the nephew sent messages of sympathy and a packet of mentholated sweets, and the maids brought cheerful chatter. When she recovered, the ladies introduced her to their favourite walks, first to the Brighton Pier and next, to the Royal Pavilion with its oriental domes and minarets; but the famous sites bustled with holiday makers. Having to endure stares which were sometimes rude, as well as unfriendly or insensitive remarks, embarrassed Sarah so that, after a few outings, she told the ladies that she preferred walking in more solitary places.

Weather permitting, she went out walking every afternoon, and finally began to apply her mind to reviewing her situation. She came to realize, with a feeling of contrition, that Lady Phipps must have felt that she was far too content to plan for her future without pressure to do so, and that the Reverend and Mrs. Schoen were too full of Christian charity to tell her the hard truths she needed to hear and absorb. To apply the necessary pressure, Lady Phipps had undertaken that difficult role and, being the kind person she was, it must have hurt her to do so. The place to which the Queen sent Sarah was the home of her sister-in-law, so it must also have been she who proposed to the Queen that Sarah be sent to Brighton for a while. Sarah smiled ruefully as she realized how successful Lady Phipps's strategy had been. Living with the inmates of the house at Clifton Hill had made it abundantly clear that, even if she succeeded in finding a position as a lady's companion, she would, indeed, find life intolerably dull. She then considered returning to Freetown to teach at the Female Institution, but rejected the idea; perhaps if they had moved to the new building she might have thought differently, but she associated the present, cramped premises with unhappiness, and besides, feared a social life centred on missionaries. She had tremendous admiration for missionaries; liked some of those she had met, even loved a few, but she feared she would find it too confining to spend all her free time among them. After her sheltered childhood and early youth, she wanted to experience more of life's possibilities; to spread her wings a little. That left marriage to Mr. Davies. Still nowhere close to accepting his proposal, she came to the conclusion that she should agree to meet him, as everyone had suggested. She would make only one condition—that the meeting take place at Palm Cottage.

She wrote to both Mrs. Schoen and Lady Phipps, informing them of her partial surrender, but the Queen had recently lost her beloved Prince Consort and was in deep mourning. It took many more weeks for her to grant Sarah permission to return to Gillingham for a weekend.

CHAPTER FOURTEEN
The Deciding Factor

Mr. James Davies came to tea at Palm Cottage on a Saturday afternoon. He looked exactly like his photograph and, as Sarah had feared, spoke in an accent that left much to be desired; but she liked his light baritone voice and his confident, yet respectful demeanour.

'So,' Mrs. Schoen said brightly, after handing round tea and sandwiches. 'Reverend Venn tells us you are into merchant shipping, Mr. Davies.'

'Yes, I am, Mrs. Schoen, though I no longer captain the ships myself. I have people working for me.'

'And what cargo do your ships carry?' Sarah asked.

'Oh, mainly agricultural produce, but any other merchandise for which there is a market. They go up and down the West African coast, buying and selling.'

Having known Frederick Forbes, and having travelled on ships herself, matters of the sea always interested Sarah. She asked James Davies what it had been like to captain his own ship; at which point Mrs. Schoen, delighted that the visit seemed to be going well, rose, smiling.

'Before you answer that, Mr. Davies, I must leave you for a while; but I'll be back before you go.'

James Davies impressed Sarah by rising to his feet at once, and giving his hostess a little bow as she made to leave the room.

'You wanted to know what it was like to be the captain of a merchant vessel...' he said when he sat down again.

'Yes. I'm sure you must have heard that my late guardian, Captain Forbes, commanded a man-of-war in the West Africa Squadron of the Royal Navy.'

'Yes, I heard that. Well, I can tell you that along the West African coast, a merchant ship was nowhere near as exciting as a man-of-war while the slave trade was going on. I taught at the CMS Grammar School in Freetown, but soon decided that teaching was not for me, so I enlisted in the Royal Navy's West Africa Squadron. It was *tremendously* exciting chasing and boarding those slave ships, and freeing our people. And I was an officer on the HMS Bloodhound, when Lagos was bombarded.'

'Lagos was bombarded?' Sarah, asked, her eyes bright with curiosity.

'Yes. Ten years ago.'

'But why?'

'At the time it was still a big slave port. The Liberated Africans, who went there from Sierra Leone, wanted the British to force the king of Lagos, Oba Kosoko, to end the slave trade. Oba Kosoko was refusing, so the Liberated Africans—"Saros", as the indigenes call us, put pressure on the British to overthrow him; which they did.'

'And you took part in the bombardment?' she asked.

'Yes, I took part in it. As a matter of fact, I was wounded and have a scar to prove it. Not long after that, I resigned from the navy and offered my services to captain a merchant vessel.'

By this time, Sarah had quite forgotten that this fascinating man was her unwelcome suitor. It was James Davies who reminded her of it by asking during in a pause in their conversation,

'Do you remember your Yoruba name?'

'Yes, it's Aina.'

'So you were born with your cord around your neck and survived;...That must mean something.'

'I don't know,' Sarah laughed. 'Perhaps.'

'If you agree to become my wife, I shall always call you that; at least in private.'

Sarah felt her cheeks grow warm.

'Is Labulo your Yoruba name?'

'Yes; it's really Olabulo, but I like the sound of J.P.L. Davies better than J.P.O. Davies...I'm quite vain, you see,' he added, with a wry smile and a twinkle in his eye.

Sarah chuckled, as she was meant to, and in that moment decided she could possibly grow fond of James Davies; at least, they would be friends, and marrying a friend would be all right. Sensing the change in her attitude, James Davies asked if he might call again.

'Yes,' Sarah said without hesitation.

They agreed on a visit in a week's time, and at the same place. During that second visit, Sarah learned that James Davies travelled to Britain on business at least twice a year, and would never dream of leaving his young wife alone in Lagos. That settled the matter. Mrs. Schoen swiftly sent the welcome news to Lady Phipps, who informed the Queen. The Queen gave Sarah permission to return to Palm Cottage, and officially approved her marriage to James Davies. Sarah went back to Clifton Hill only to collect her belongings and to thank Miss Welsh, and the other inmates of the house for their hospitality.

PART SIX
Sarah Bonetta Davies

CHAPTER FIFTEEN
A Wedding Like No Other

60, Burton Crescent,
Bloomsbury,
London.
21st August, 1862.

Dear Miss Sass,

Please forgive this very long silence. I was in a state of mental torment for almost a year. The reasons for it are complex, but you will probably have a good idea what it was partly about when I tell you that on the fourteenth of August, I became Sarah Bonetta DAVIES. My husband, Mr. James Davies, is the son of Liberated Africans. He was born in Bathurst Village in Sierra Leone and educated at the CMS Grammar School; in that regard, we are equally yoked. He is a businessman—quite wealthy it appears, but he has also done missionary work, and tells me he visited the Female Institution during the time I was there. He remembers you very well; but I have no recollection of that visit, nor does he remember seeing me, so it must have taken place while I was confined to bed with one of my feverish colds. We shall be relocating to Freetown as soon as it can be arranged, and he has agreed that, as you once suggested, I teach at the Female Institution until we start a family.

I shall never ever forget my wedding day. It took place at St. Nicholas Church in Brighton. The weather could have been kinder; but that did not matter in the least. I felt surrounded by love as I entered the church, and for the first time, beautiful. So many of the friends I had made over the years were present and waiting at the entrance to greet me. The Queen had had made for me the most gorgeous wedding gown imaginable for someone not of European royalty. It was white silk with white trimming, and my veil was held in place by a wreath of orange blossoms, very similar to what her own daughters wore at their weddings. When my friends and mothers told me in whispers that I looked beautiful, for the first time, I felt like a princess. My bridesmaids entered the church before me. The first four were Africans, one of them my husband's sister. They, too, wore white gowns, but with red trim. The

next four were English, their white gowns
trimmed with blue. The next four were African,
and the next four English—sixteen in all. Sweet
little flower girls followed them. Captain Forbes's
brother walked me up the aisle and gave me away,
which made me rather tearful. I hope you don't
think me ungrateful, but I so wished it could have
been his brother.

It was very much a CMS wedding.
Reverend Venn, whom you know well, and a
Liberated African clergyman, Reverend Nichol,
assisted Bishop Beckles, who officiated. I'm sure
you are acquainted with him as well. The church
bells pealed when we were pronounced man and
wife, and a huge cheer went up as we walked out
of the church. It seemed like the whole of
Brighton had come to see the unusual spectacle
of a black bride and groom, as well as elegantly
dressed English men and women, mingling easily
with Africans, equally elegant in their attire. We
left for London on the five o'clock train, after a
sumptuous wedding breakfast. Oh, that was a
joyful day, Miss Sass. As for married life, so far, I
am finding it satisfactory.

I was so very sorry to hear that the walls of the new school building fell down, due to bad workmanship. What a crushing blow that must have been! I praise the Almighty that you have found the courage and strength to start again and not abandon an endeavour which must be taking a great toll on your health, especially in that deadly climate.

Expect to see us before long.

<u>24th August</u>

An unfortunate incident occurred before I could complete my letter to you. I began to smell smoke coming from one of the rooms and my husband went to investigate. Indeed there was a fire, though its cause was a mystery as it happened in the middle of the day. We raised the alarm and fire engines arrived quickly and confined it to just the one room. Thanking God that not much damage had been done, we heaved sighs of relief. Imagine our horrified disbelief when, as night fell, another fire broke out, this one much more serious. Despite the efforts of the firemen, part of the roof burned away, and it ruined several rooms on the upper storey before it could be contained. To make matters worse, water from the fire hoses, severely damaged the rooms and furnishings below. The next day, the *London Times* raised the possibility of arson. We found that most disturbing, for it was a sharp reminder that not all English people are kindly disposed to Africans in their midst, no matter how respectable they might be.

Needless to say, the incident cast something of shadow over our honeymoon; but that has not stopped us from carrying on with our plans, and from having an enjoyable time as we get to know each other. Because of the fire we are going to be of no fixed abode until our departure, so please keep any questions you may have till we meet again. We shall sail for Freetown shortly.

Yours very affectionately,
Sarah B. Davies.

CHAPTER SIXTEEN
Saro Woman

Broad Street,
Lagos.
20th, November, 1863.

Dear Miss Sass,

I am sorry that I could spend only a few months helping you out at the school. I did not expect that I would so soon become 'with child'. I had hoped to return after our baby's birth, but James decided that business opportunities would be better in Lagos, and that we should go and settle there without delay. I was greatly disappointed that you were away on leave so that I could not say goodbye.

I am fairly settled in Lagos now. I was surprised to discover that it is a large island in a lagoon. We live in an area known as Saro Town. It is called that because we are all Yorubas, who immigrated from Sierra Leone. The indigenes call us 'Saros'. Not all of them have welcomed us, but those that have—the majority—say our presence has brought them education, and introduced them to modern ways. Those who have embraced Christianity, also credit Saros with bringing them to Christ. In another section of the town live people known as Agudas—Yorubas, who were once slaves in Brazil, but decided to return home when they became free. Unlike Saros, who are generally close to being black, they are of every shade, from a very dark brown, to beige. We do not mix socially; for one thing, they don't speak English; for another, they are mostly Roman Catholics, and for another, though greatly skilled, to judge from the astonishingly beautiful houses they build in their quarter, they are mostly artisans— carpenters, masons, painters and such.

I received permission from the Queen to call our daughter Victoria. She went further; offered to be her godmother, and sent her as a christening present, a gold cup with a salver, and a knife, fork and spoon. The cup and salver are inscribed: to Victoria Davies, from her godmother, Victoria, Queen of Great Britain and Ireland, 1863. We feel deeply honoured to have what will, no doubt, become an heirloom.

There is quite a social scene in Lagos, but until I stop nursing Victoria, my own life has to remain fairly quiet. I sing solos in church occasionally, and teach Sunday School; that's about it. James's time is much taken up with business, and service to the community. He is good friends with Reverend Samuel Crowther, and together they have undertaken several worthy projects. He is proving to be a kind, considerate husband, *and* he makes me laugh, for which I give thanks.

Affectionately yours,
Sarah Davies.

--

Broad street,
Lagos,
6th September, 1865.

Dear Miss Sass,

I was absolutely delighted to read in your recent letter that the new Female Institution has been officially opened, but was sad to read that you were not well enough to stay for the whole ceremony. You have obviously been working far too hard. I do hope you are taking life easier now that the work is done. I greatly appreciated your sending me a sketch of the building and its grounds. It looks splendid; and I am sure it will bring a bit of England to Freetown once the field in front of the building is covered with well cut grass and the round garden is in full bloom. I salute your achievement, dear Miss Sass. You will surely receive an honourable mention in the annals of the Church Missionary Society and of the Female Institution; and well deserved that will be. You have been a blessing to West Africa.

You must have heard that the Reverend Samuel Crowther has been ordained a bishop of the Anglican Church—the first African to be so honoured. We, Saros, are extremely proud of his achievement. He and my husband have established a social and cultural centre called The Academy, where I sometimes sing and play the piano at concerts. James is also involved with setting up a CMS grammar school in Lagos. As I said in another letter, he is committed to improving our community, bless him.

Always with affection,

Sarah Bonetta Davies.

Broad Street
Lagos,
3rd February, 1868.

Dear Miss Sass,

I recently returned from England and while there, took Victoria with me to visit her godmother, the Queen. Even if I say so myself, she is a charming and intelligent child, so I wasn't surprised that Her Majesty was taken with her, though she said, 'She's far blacker than you, isn't she?' which I thought quite unnecessary. She gave her a gold bracelet and told me she would be responsible for her fees at the Cheltenham Ladies College when the time comes. Can you imagine that, Miss Sass? My daughter attending one of the best schools for girls in Britain. Truly, Her

Majesty's generosity overwhelms me. I didn't always appreciate her taking me under her wing when I was younger, but now realize that her doing so was one of my greatest blessings.

Yours most affectionately,
Sarah Davies.

The Female Institution,
Kissy Road,
Freetown.
18th September, 1871.

Dear Miss Sass,

Thank you for your letter.

We now have a son called Arthur and Sickly Sarah is enjoying much better health. James says that is because motherhood suits me. I am helping out here for a few weeks as there has been much illness among the European staff.

I am so impressed with the new school building. The red stone adds dignity to its excellent architecture. I'm sure you must have heard that, in recognition of the generosity of the dear people who made possible this magnificent building, some of us, former pupils of the Female Institution, have become advocates for renaming it the Annie Walsh Memorial School. I hope that happens soon.

I must say that the school is not the same without you; but I know you could not stay any longer. For twenty years you gave your all in the Lord's vineyard, without counting the cost, and now deserve to rest. I pray that you enjoy many years of a healthy and peaceful retirement.

Yours affectionately,
Sarah Davies.

--

Broad Street,
Lagos.
1st October, 1975.

Dear Miss Sass,

I hope this finds you well, and that the pain in your knees has lessened enough for you to have enjoyed your garden this summer.

I was again in England recently, but it was a brief and depressing visit. We contacted only one or two of our closest friends as we were in no mood for light conversations. The reason for our visit was that most of James's businesses have run into financial difficulties, resulting in his being pursued by creditors, and in danger of being declared bankrupt. That would be a terrible humiliation for a man of such good character and who, until recently, was a member of the Legislative Council. I have been more pained by the attitude of some people here, whom we thought were friends, than by our perilous situation. James has been kind and generous to everyone, thinking it his Christian duty, but now that he needs support, many of the people he helped are saying things about him that are malicious and untrue, all due to simmering jealousy, I suspect. At no time in my life have the words of that lovely hymn, 'Begone unbelief,' meant more to me. Over and over again I say to myself,

His love in times past,
Forbids me to think
He'll leave me at last
In trouble to sink.

However, there has been some sunshine amid all the gloom. We have yet another addition to our family—a daughter whom we have named, Stella. Unfortunately, her arrival has disproved James's theory that becoming a mother was good for my health. Perhaps it's the great stress I have been under, but I seem to spend more time in bed than out of it these days—my usual feverish colds and chestiness. But I am decidedly better this week, hence I have sufficient energy to catch up with my correspondence.

We now have rickshaws in Lagos, and I suppose they have also appeared on the streets of Freetown. What a difference it makes not having to go everywhere on foot. I wish I were well enough to enjoy them more, though I do feel for the men who drag them, especially when their passengers are heavier than the average.

May God continue to shower blessings on you.

Always affectionately,
Sarah Bonetta Davies.

Broad Street,
Lagos,
2nd April, 1878.

Dear Miss Sass,

Thank you so much for your very kind letter. Unfortunately, I have been quite ill again. Poor James is beside himself with worry—as if he hasn't enough to worry about with his legal tangles and financial woes. The court cases are not going very well; but we continue to trust in God's mercy to see us through.

I wonder if you have heard the good news that our advocacy has won the day? From henceforth, the Female Institution will be known as the Annie Walsh Memorial School. That news gave me such a lift that I tried to sing the Doxology but began to cough and grew too short of breath to complete even that short hymn. I wonder if I'll ever be able to sing again.

Please remember us in your prayers.

Affectionately,
Sarah Davies.

CHAPTER SEVENTEEN
Journey's End

Royal Edinburgh Hotel,
Funchal,
Madeira.
29th April, 1880.

Dear Miss Sass,

I am afraid my health worsened since my last letter; in fact I nearly passed away last January. I developed a hacking cough which nothing could relieve; even my throat suffered on account of my constant hard coughing. Our family doctor finally diagnosed consumption, upon which James insisted that I come here at once, since Madeira's climate has the reputation of being conducive to recovery from lung ailments. The specialist I have consulted here has assured me that if I follow his instructions, I shall be up and about in six months. My present condition makes it hard for me to believe that, but for my children and my husband's sakes, I obey him, and pray for the best.

The other day I met a Mrs. Burton from the Female Institution (the Annie Walsh now). She is here on leave, which made me wonder whether you ever spent any of your own leaves here. It isn't all that warm at this time of year, but I've been able to take a couple of carriage drives. I enjoyed the beauty of the island; apart from delightful sea views and an abundance of lovely flowers, rather like Freetown, tree-covered mountains are visible in every direction.

My nurse maid and the two youngest children are here with me, but the doctor has warned me to avoid close contact to protect them from becoming infected. That makes me so sad. Victoria is already at Cheltenham Ladies College, and doing very well.

Dear Miss Sass, just in case, thank you so much for your friendship which has been constant since the day I met you at Government Wharf in Freetown. You always encouraged me to do my very best, so I know I must have disappointed you from time to time; but I did do my best. Thank you from the bottom of my heart.

> With the warmest affection,
> Sarah Bonetta Davies.

Sarah spent her days on a sofa by the window in her hotel room. It had a backrest, which eased her coughing, and in that half-sitting position she could see both the distant mountains and the array of gorgeous flowers in the hotel's gardens. After six weeks in Funchal, she had come to the conclusion that her health was not improving, nor was it likely to, for she felt herself growing weaker by the day. The time came when she lacked the energy to write more than a few lines to her husband. Then, she found she could not hold up a book long enough to complete a short chapter, which meant reading her leather-bound Bible was out of the question; and she could no longer do any of the marking she used to enjoy. But her mind remained active, and she was not in much pain so, in between naps, she spent the slow hours reflecting on her life.

She marvelled at the coincidence that had shaped her destiny: had Captain Forbes come to Abomey one year earlier, he would not have been present to rescue her; but he did come then, which led to her first contact with Queen Victoria, the Church Missionary Society, and all that followed, including her marriage to James Davies. Her husband had become very dear to her, and except for the last few turbulent years, they had shared not only a comfortable life of service to a community to which they both fully belonged, but had also had three delightful children. The arrival of Victoria, Arthur and Stella had brought such joy to their lives, especially the last two, coming as they did, eight and ten years after Victoria. I have been so blessed, Sarah thought, yet could not help grieving that her life was about to end before her children grew up, and at a time when James was in trouble. With court cases pending, it seemed highly unlikely that he would be able to visit her before the end which she instinctively felt was near. And Victoria. To think that when I left her at school that would be the last time we would see each other. She wept a little then, but soon drifted off to sleep.

Eventually, even moving from her bed to the sofa became too much for her. The doctor brought in a woman, who knew a little English, to nurse her. Sarah's one activity, if one could call it that, was feebly blowing kisses to her children when the nursemaid brought them to the door in the mornings. Her memories became more random and fragmented as she faded—those rides in the cold with Princess Alice, the Queen stroking the scars on her cheeks and asking what they meant. Rebecca Leigh plaiting her hair. I wonder what became of her, she thought drowsily. Bowlegged Tommy Clegg, who first taught her English. She smiled, remembering how she had tried and failed to whistle like him. Those walks to and from St. George's Cathedral on Sundays; strange that the first bishop was the man who baptized her in Badagry—Reverend Vidal. Mrs. Vidal painting her portrait, Mrs. Cole's beef stew; Mahoussi—wailing when she thought she was going to be killed, waving goodbye after Captain Forbes saved her life; her mother singing as she tackled her hair… On the

13th of August, she slipped into coma from which she did not emerge, and on the 15th, the doctor pronounced her dead.

The British consul in Madeira arranged for the Davies children and their nursemaid to be repatriated to Lagos, but kept Sarah's box of expensive jewelry as security till her husband paid outstanding debts for hotel lodging, medical care, sending her children home, and her funeral expenses. James Davies collected them sometime after Sarah's burial and took the opportunity to ask the doctor about the circumstances of her death.

'Did she say anything before she lost consciousness?'

'Yes. According to the nurse who called me, Mrs. Davies said very clearly, 'Tomorrow…James's birthday.''

On hearing that, James Davies covered his face with both hands for a minute, breathing heavily; then he took out a spotless white handkerchief and dried his wet cheeks.

'The fourteenth of August was also our eighteenth wedding anniversary,' he said, and went on, 'Oh, Aina... She didn't deserve to die alone.'

'Aina?' said the doctor, 'I thought Mrs. Davies's name was Sarah.'

'That was the name she received at her baptism. Her real name was Aina.'

EPILOGUE

Aina's remains lie in the English Cemetery in Funchal, Madeira.

The preacher at her memorial service in Lagos fondly remembered her willingness to serve, her lively personality, her lovely speaking and singing voice and accomplished piano playing; and a Lagos newspaper described her as, 'one of Africa's brightest ornaments.'

James Davies eventually recovered from his legal and financial woes and had a huge granite obelisk erected in her memory on his vast cocoa plantation at Ijon, on the west side of Lagos. He remarried; but not for another nine years. Victoria Davies completed her schooling at the Cheltenham Ladies College and continued to visit her royal namesake and godmother, Queen Victoria, from time to time. The Queen later provided her with a lifetime annuity of forty pounds—quite a substantial sum in those days. She married Dr. John Randle, an eminent 'Saro' physician and political activist. Miss Julia Sass passed away in 1891.

AUTHOR'S NOTE

Sarah Forbes Bonetta's story is fairly well known in Britain. Captain Frederick Forbes's 1851 publication, *Dahomey and the Dahomans*, provided an account of her rescue from King Ghezo's court and his early impressions of her. Walter Dean Myers's biography for young adults, *At Her Majesty's Request*, provided further details of her life story, as did Caroline Bressey's, *Of Africa's brightest: a Short Biography of Sarah Forbes Bonetta.* My own research unearthed additional details of her life and background and answered some remaining questions, but not all, hence my decision to use my poetic licence to create characters and scenes as necessary for the purposes of the story. Sarah's life before she was kidnapped, the names of Frederick Forbes's children as well as scenes from her life with the family are all products of my imagination, as are the description of her first visit to Queen Victoria, her years at the Female Institution and her reason for leaving it. Her conversations with Mrs. Schoen and Lady Phipps in connection with Mr. James Davies's proposal of marriage, how she finally decided to marry him and her last days, are all fiction; and so are her letters to Miss Sass, though most of the information they contain is factual.